U0079378

HOW DO YOU DO

最實用的生活英語

DAILY ENGLISH

國家圖書館出版品預行編目資料

How do you do最實用的生活英語 / 張瑜凌編著
-- 三版. -- 新北市 : 雅典文化, 民109.01
面 ; 公分. -- (全民學英文 ; 53)
ISBN 978-986-97795-8-6(平裝附光碟片)

1.英語 2.句法 3.會話

805.169 108019352

全民學英文系列 53

How do you do最實用的生活英語

編著／張瑜凌
責任編輯／賴美君
美術編輯／王國卿
封面設計／林鈺恆

法律顧問：方圓法律事務所／涂成樞律師

總經銷：永續圖書有限公司
永續圖書線上購物網
www.foreverbooks.com.tw

CVS代理／美璟文化有限公司
TEL：(02) 2723-9968
FAX：(02) 2723-9668

出版日／2020年01月

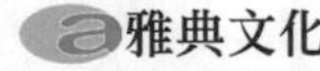

出版社
22103 新北市汐止區大同路三段194號9樓之1
TEL (02) 8647-3663
FAX (02) 8647-3660

track 001

★ Are you ready?

準備好了嗎？

深入分析

詢問對方「準備好了嗎？」可以說"Are you ready?"，除了是表示你自己已經準備好要行動、要出發，也是一種催促對方「快一點」的用語，例如："Ready?"（準備好了嗎？）

也可以在"ready"的後面加上"to＋原形動詞"的句型，表示「準備去做某事」的意思，例如："Are you ready to pain the fence?"，表示「你準備好要去油漆圍籬了嗎？」

實用會話

Ⓐ Are you ready?
準備好了嗎？

Ⓑ Ready.
準備好了！

Ⓐ OK, let's go.
好，我們走吧！

實用會話

Ⓐ Ready?
準備好了嗎？

Ⓑ Sure. I am ready.
當然！我準備好了

track 002

★He told me so much about you.

他告訴過我很多關於你的事。

深入分析

若是經由某人的介紹而認識新朋友，而且你常常聽他提起這位新朋友，你就可以告訴新朋友："He told me so much about you."，表示「他告訴過我很多關於你的事」，這句話非常適合當成和新朋友打開話匣子的用語。

而中文常說的「久仰大名」，則可以說："I've heard a lot about you."也和上一句有異曲同工之妙，只是沒有特別說明從哪裡得知對方的消息。

實用會話

Ⓐ Nice to meet you, Carol.
卡蘿，很高興認識妳！

Ⓑ Me too. Eric told me so much about you.
我也是！艾瑞克告訴我很多關於你的事。

Ⓐ I hope nothing bad.
希望不是壞事！

實用會話

Ⓐ Good to see you, Sandy.
珊蒂，真高興見到妳！

Ⓑ I've heard so much about you.
我聽說很多關於你的事！

track 003

★It'll be fun.

會很好玩的！

深入分析

若是你想要說服對方一起參加某個活動，對方卻擔心可能會很無聊（boring）而猶疑不決是否要同行時，你就可以告訴對方："It'll be fun."，表示「會很好玩的！」，這句話透露出一種預期心態，表示「不用擔心會冷場，一定會很好玩，不去可是很可惜喔！」的意味。

實用會話

A I don't wanna go.

我不想去！

B Come on. It'll be fun.

一起來嘛！會很好玩的！

A Well, I'll think about it.

嗯，我會考慮看看！

衍生例句

▶ I'll make it fun.

我會讓這件事變得很好玩的！

track 004

★It's not so bad, right?

事情沒那麼糟，對吧？

深入分析

"so bad"是表示「情況如此糟糕」的意思，而若是你發覺事情沒有大家想像中那樣的令人沮喪，或是事情還有轉圜、拯救的餘地時，你就可以打圓場地說："It's not so bad."，表示事情還是有希望的，以此激起在場所有人的希望或鬥志！

實用會話

A It's not so bad, right?

A Thank you for coming over.
謝謝你趕過來！

B I'm sorry about the whole thing.
對這整件事我感到很遺憾！

A It's not so bad, right?
事情沒那麼糟，對吧？

B I don't think so.
我才不會這麼認為。

實用會話

A So bad?
有很糟嗎？

B Sorry, sir. We did our best.
抱歉，先生，我們盡力了！

track 005

★What can it hurt?

又沒什麼損失！

深入分析

對一個畏畏縮縮、舉棋不定、猶豫不決的人來說，唯有當頭棒喝的提醒才能夠督促對方勇敢地做出行動或決定，此時你就可以說"What can it hurt?"，表示「又沒什麼損失，你不用害怕！」的意思，也是藉此讓對方能更勇敢、更果決！

實用會話

Ⓐ What did she say?
她的建議是什麼呢？

Ⓑ I don't know. I just don't want to ask her.
我不知道！我就是不想要求她。

Ⓐ Hey, man, what can it hurt?
嘿，老兄，又沒什麼損失！

衍生例句

▶ That won't hurt.
又沒壞處！

track 006

★That's a good question.

問得好！

深入分析

若是對方提出一個很好的問題，你就可以讚賞對方："That's a good question."，中文就是「問得好！」表示認同對方的問題、也欣賞對方提問的水準。此外，你也可以只是簡單地說："Good question."

實用會話

A It would become your number one priority. Right?

那會是你的首要任務，對吧？

B I don't think so. Why don't we just leave it alone?

才不是！不要管它不就好了？

A That's a good question.

問得好！

track 007

★Agree?

同意嗎？

深入分析

詢問對方是否同意、認同、接受建議的最簡單問句就是"Agree?"，中文就是「你同意吧？」，完整的問句則是"Do you agree?"。若是要特別說明「同意某人」，則可以說："I agree with you."，表示「我和你的想法是一致的」。

若是「我絕不同意」，則可以說"I couldn't agree less."

實用會話

A Agree?

同意嗎？

B You've got it.

沒錯！

衍生例句

▶ I agree.

我同意。

▶ I couldn't agree more.

我完全同意！

▶ We're all for it.

我們全都同意。

▶ Whatever I said, he'd disagree.

不論我說什麼，他都不會同意。

track 008

★ Don't be like that.

不要這樣嘛！

深入分析

不認同對方的行為或是希望對方不要再有這種言行舉止時，你都可以直接的表明："Don't be like that."，中文意思就是「不要這樣嘛！」，表示你不希望再看見對方的這種反應或行為。

實用會話

Ⓐ Can we talk?

我們可以聊一聊嗎？

Ⓑ Sure. What's up?

好啊！怎麼啦？

Ⓐ It's about Jim and my wife...

是有關吉姆和我太太的事⋯

Ⓑ Come on. Don't be like that.

振作點！不要這樣嘛！

track 009

★ You look upset.

你看起來很沮喪！

深入分析

"someone look like＋形容詞"是表示「某人看起來很像…」的陳述，是一種關心對方現況的常用語句，能夠幫助你和對方建立起特殊情誼的寒暄語句，例如：

☑You look terrible.你看起來臉色不太好！
☑You look happy.你看起來很高興！
☑You look angry.你看起來很生氣！
☑She looks pale.她看起來臉色蒼白！

實用會話

Ⓐ You look upset. Are you OK?
你看起來很沮喪，你還好嗎？

Ⓑ I don't know.
不知道耶！

Ⓐ What happened?
怎麼啦？

Ⓑ I can't leave my business alone that often.
我不能經常放著我的事業不管！

track 010

★ Are you OK?

你還好吧？

深入分析

如何建立人際關係？很簡單，主動付出你的關心。當你看見對方臉色不好、氣色不佳時，不妨主動關心朋友，問問對方"Are you OK?"，也許因為你主動釋出的關心，能夠讓對方獲得幫助或發洩一下情緒。

實用會話

Ⓐ Are you OK? You look terrible.

你還好吧？你看起來臉色不太好！

Ⓑ I have a headache.

我頭疼。

Ⓐ I think you've caught a cold.

我想你是得了感冒。

實用會話

Ⓐ There you are. Are you OK? I came down as soon as I heard something.

你在這裡喔！你還好吧？我聽到聲音就下來看看！

Ⓑ I've been trying to reach you.

我一直在找你。

衍生例句

▶ Are you all right?

你還好吧？

track 011

★How do you feel now?

你現在覺得如何？

深入分析

當對方不舒服或生病中，你就可以關心對方目前的狀況："How do you feel now?"，意思是：「你現在覺得如何？」

實用會話

A David?
大衛嗎？

B Hi, Sandy.
嗨，珊蒂！

A How do you feel now?
你現在覺得如何？

B Terrible. My feet are killing me.
糟透了！我的腳好痛喔！

實用會話

A How do you feel now?
你現在覺得如何？

B I don't know. I feel painful when I touch it.
不知道耶！我摸的時候會很痛！

衍生例句

▶ How are you feeling now?
你現在感覺如何？

track 012

★I don't have time.

我沒有時間！

深入分析

時間稍縱即逝，所以我們要把握當下的時間，當某件事花掉你太多時間時，你就可以說："I don't have time."

「時間」(time) 是不可數名詞，「花太多時間」是"too much time"，不可以說成："too many time"。

實用會話

A Why don't you keep learning it?
你為什麼不繼續學？

B I don't have time.
我沒有時間！

A Time. It's always about time, isn't it?
時間！總是時間的問題，對嗎？

衍生例句

▶That's too much time.
花太多時間了。

▶I have no time.
我沒有時間！

track 013

★I would if I had time.

如果有時間的話，我會的。

深入分析

「沒有時間」的英文該怎麼說？很簡單，只要說："I have no time."，若是對方問你是否願意做某事時，你可以回答：「若是我有時間，我會…」，英文就是："I would if I had time."。

實用會話

A Would you like to come over?

你會過來嗎？

B I would if I had time.

如果有時間我會的。

A I see. Call me if you decide to come over.

我瞭解了！如果你決定要過來，打電話給我！

實用會話

A Would you buy some milk on your way home?

可以請你回家的時候順便買一些牛奶嗎？

B I would if I had time.

如果有時間的話我會的。

track 014

★You can't please everyone.

你無法討好每一個人。

深入分析

沒有人願意得罪人，但是你也無法討好所有的人，此時英文就叫做："You can't please everyone."，表示你只要盡力、對得起自己就好了，可不要為了討好所有人而搞得「豬八戒照鏡子，裡外不是人」喔！

實用會話

A She's gonna hate me forever.

她會恨我一輩子的！

B You can't please everyone.

你無法討好每一個人。

A What shall I do now?

我現在應該怎麼辦？

B You tell me.

你說呢？

track 015

★This is about us now.

現在這是我們之間的事了！

深入分析

「這是我們之間的恩怨，不關第三者的事」，這麼一大串中文的英文說法要怎麼說呢？聽好，就叫做："This is about us now."，是不是很簡單？沒有任何艱澀的單字就把一串中文翻譯成英文囉！「不關第三者的事」雖然沒有出現在句子中，但這就是不同語言之間有趣之處，在相同的情境下就可以有相同的意思啊！

實用會話

A I didn't mean it.

我不是有心的！

B I know. But this is about us now.

我知道，但是現在這是我們之間的事了！

A Hey, would you forgive me?

嘿，你願意原諒我嗎？

B I don't think so.

我是不會原諒你的！

track 016

★ Not once.

一次都沒有！

深入分析

若是對方問你：「是否曾經…」，而你的回答是「一次都沒有！」，就可以說："Not once."，也就是表示「從未」（never）的意思，反義的說法則為："many times"（很多次）。

實用會話

A Have you ever bought her flowers?

你有送過花給她嗎？

B Not once.

一次都沒有！

A Why not?

為什麼不送？

B It's a long story.

說來話長。

track 017

★ It's not funny, OK?

一點都不好玩，好嗎？

深入分析

若是有人玩笑開過頭，或是行為幼稚到不行，你都可以說："It's not funny, OK?"（一點都不好玩，好嗎？），表示你不欣賞對方的言行，有制止、不認同的意味存在。

你還可以用反諷的語氣問對方："Is this some kind of joke?"，表示「你是開玩笑的吧？」

實用會話

Ⓐ It doesn't make sense.

這不合常理！

Ⓑ Come on, it's just a joke.

不要這樣嘛！只是開個玩笑罷了！

Ⓐ It's not funny, OK?

一點都不好玩，好嗎？

實用會話

Ⓐ David, this is so cool. Check this out.

大衛，很酷喔！你看！

Ⓑ Is this some kind of joke?

這是什麼完笑話嗎？

track 018

★Funny.

有趣喔！

深入分析

若是你聽見一個有趣、好玩的事情時，口語中文會說：「好好玩！」或是「真有趣！」若是用英文表達，就可以說："Funny."，完整的句子則是 "It's funny."

此外，"funny"有的時候也可以形容人："He's a funny guy."表示「他這個人相當有趣、幽默」的意思。

實用會話

Ⓐ I used to be a lot stronger.

我過去比較壯！

Ⓑ You mean when you were young?

你是說你年輕的時候嗎？

Ⓐ Funny, I thought I still was.

有趣喔！我以為我還是(很年輕)啊！

實用會話

Ⓐ Come over here. See?

你過來！你看！

Ⓑ Hmm, it's funny.

嗯，很有趣！

A No, it's not! It's weird, isn't it?

不是，才不是！是很詭異，不是嗎？

實用會話

A Maybe that's why he broke up with me.

也許這就是為什麼他和我分手吧！

B You're funny.

你真是幽默喔！

track 019

★ You're kidding me.

你別拿我開玩笑了！

深入分析

若是對方對你開個無傷大雅的小玩笑，可千萬不要生氣喔，別當個開不起玩笑的人喔，你只要回應對方："You're kidding me."，表示「你別消遣我了！」

實用會話

A What do you think of this one?

你覺得這個怎麼樣？

B Oh, you're kidding me.

哦，你別拿我開玩笑了！

A Hey, I'm serious.

嘿，我是正經的！

衍生例句

► Are you kidding?

你在開玩笑吧？

► This joke has gone a little too far.

這個玩笑開得有點過分了。

► He can't take a joke.

他開不得玩笑。

track 020

★ Fine.

隨便你！

深入分析

若有人屢勸不聽，不理會你的苦口婆心，仍舊執意要獨斷獨行，你就可以說："Fine."，可別以為這是鼓掌叫好、讚美的意思，反而是指「好，隨便你，你自己要負責喔！」瞧，只要一個英文單字，就說明了這麼多的中文意思，英文真的很簡單吧！

實用會話

A He doesn't care about you at all.

他一點都不在乎你啊！

B Maybe I have to go with him.

也許我應該和他一起去！

Ⓐ Fine. I don't think it will lead to a good result.
隨便你！我認為這事不會有什麼好結果。

實用會話

Ⓐ I've changed my mind.
我已經改變主意了！

Ⓑ Fine. It's none of my business.
隨便你！不關我的事！

track 021

★ Suit yourself.
隨你高興！

深入分析

當對方下決定之後，你雖然不認同，但也莫可奈何時，仍舊可以發洩情緒地說："Suit yourself."，表示「你要自己負責」的意思。

實用會話

Ⓐ What would you like to have?
你想吃什麼？

Ⓑ How about this one?
這個好嗎？

Ⓐ You want a pizza with pineapple on it? OK, suit yourself.
你想吃有鳳梨的披薩？好啊！隨你高興！

徹底學會英文

Fine.
隨便你！

隨然你不認同對方的決定，你仍可以用反面諷刺的方式回答：「好，隨便你」，看似稱讚，卻沒有任何欣賞之意，英文就叫做："Fine."

A：I quit.
我放棄了！

B：Fine.
隨便你！

track 022

★ Does it make any different?

有差別嗎？

深入分析

若要在兩者之間做出選擇，偏偏這兩種選擇會讓人舉棋不定、猶疑不決，該怎麼辦呢？可以求助旁人："Does it make any different?"，表示你實在不知道該在這兩者（或更多）之間做出最好的選擇，所以希望能夠知道兩者之間的差別在哪裡。

實用會話

A Do I have to finish it by tomorrow?
我明天前就要完成嗎？

B Does it make any different?
有差別嗎？

A Sure. I'm really exhausted now.
當然有差啊！我現在累斃了！

衍生例句

▶ That makes no difference.
這沒什麼區別。

track 023

★ Let me guess.

我來猜猜！

深入分析

當你收到神秘的禮物時，若是有人想要透露給你禮物內容時，就趕緊阻止對方："Don't tell me. Let me guess.，表示「不要告訴我，讓我來猜猜！」

此外，假如好友神秘地說她交了一位你認識的帥哥男友，你也可以說："Let me guess."，對方就會知道你不希望她先告訴你是哪一號人物！

實用會話

A Here's a gift for you.
這裡有個禮物送給你。

B Let me guess. It's a book, isn't it?
我來猜猜！是書對嗎？

A Good guess.

猜得真準！

實用會話

A You know what? I'm seeing someone.

你知道嗎？我已經有交往的對象了！

B Let me guess. Is it Jim?

我來猜猜！是吉姆嗎？

A How do you know about it?

你怎麼會知道？

track 024

★ Guess what?

猜猜看？

深入分析

"Guess what?"雖然是「猜猜看？」的意思，但卻不一定非得要對方猜測，而是在告訴對方某件事之前，一種習慣性的用語，有點類似中文的「你知道嗎？」的用法，後面所說的內容才是你希望告知對方的重點。

實用會話

A How are you doing, Jim?

吉姆，你好嗎？

B Guess what? I passed my math exam.

你知道嗎？我的數學考試通過了！

A Congratulations.

恭喜你喔！

實用會話

A What were you doing here?

你在這裡幹嘛？

B Never mind. Guess what?

這不重要！你猜猜看發生什麼事？

A You tell me.

你就直接說吧！

track 025

★ Check this out.

你來看看！

深入分析

check是檢查、審視的意思，但若是想要給朋友看某個新玩意，你就可以說："Check this out."，表示邀請他一起分享這個好玩的新玩意的意思，直接一點的說法你也可以說："Take a look"，表示中文「你看看！」的意思。

實用會話

A Hi, buddy. Check this out.

嗨，兄弟！你來看看！

Ⓑ What is it?

這是什麼？

Ⓐ It's an MP3.

這是個MP3播放器。

衍生例句

▶ Take a look at this.

你來看看！

track 026

★ You'll check out the rest, won't you?

你會檢查剩下的部份，對嗎？

深入分析

"check out"是常用片語，表示「確認」、「檢驗」的意思，是藉由檢驗所得的線索，要尋找和答案或事實相關的蛛絲馬跡，例如當大家都有聽見屋外有怪聲音時，你就可以提議出去看看發生什麼事，此時就可以說"Let's check it out."

實用會話

Ⓐ Let's head upstairs.

我們上樓去吧！

Ⓑ You'll check out the rest, won't you?

你們會檢查剩下的部分，對嗎？

A No. Maybe we should get out of here.

不會！也許我們應該要離開這裡！

track 027

★This is serious.

事情很嚴重！

深入分析

若是發生很嚴重(serious)的事情，而對方仍舊是一派嘻皮笑臉、不正經，你就可以嚴正地告訴對方這件事的嚴重性："This is serious."，表示「這件事是嚴肅的，我是正經地看待這件事」，希望對方的態度也能夠端正一些。此外，也可以應用在人當主詞的句型"I'm serious."表示「我是正經的」。

實用會話

A Why don't you just leave it alone?

你就不要管啦！

B Hey, this is serious.

嘿，事情很嚴重！

A Come on, it's just a joke.

不要這樣嘛！開個玩笑而已啊！

實用會話

A I'm serious.

我是認真的！

B OK. I'll do what you said.

好吧！我就照你說的做！

track 028

★I have faith in you.

我對你有信心！

深入分析

若是兒子對即將參加的比賽沒有信心(faith)，老是擔心自己的實力不足，你就可以為他加油打氣，鼓勵他盡力就好，你對他是有信心的："I have faith in you."。

此外，英文是沒有「得失心」的說法，所以若是希望對方不要有太大的得失心，只要「盡力就好」，英文就叫做"Do your best."

實用會話

A Shall I do it on my own?

我應該要自己做嗎？

B Baby, I have faith in you.

寶貝，我對你有信心！

A You do?

你真的對我有信心？

track 029

★How sweet.

你真是貼心！

深入分析

只要是對方做了貼心的事，例如：記得你的生日、幫你解決問題、站在你的立場替你考慮問題，舉凡這種令人感到窩心的行為等，你都可以在"Thank you."之外，再稱讚對方："How sweet."，對象不論是男女都適用，是一句非常好用的感激用語。

實用會話

A Let me help you with it.
我來幫你！

B How sweet. Thank you.
你真是貼心！謝謝！

A No problem.
不客氣！

實用會話

A I'll walk you home.
我陪你散步回家！

B How sweet you are.
你真是貼心！

track 030

★ That's very kind of you.

你真是好心！

深入分析

當對方有善意的行為、言語時，你除了感謝（Thank you）之外，還可以讓對方知道你的感謝是因為對方的好心腸，中文常說：「你真是好心！」英文就叫做"That's very kind of you."

實用會話

A Here, let me help you with it.

來，我幫你！

B Oh, thanks. That's very kind of you.

喔，謝謝！你真是好心！

實用會話

A Here you are.

給你！

B Thank you so much. That's very kind of you.

真是太謝謝你了！你真是好心！

衍生例句

► You're so nice.

= How nice you are.

= How nice of you.

你真是好心！

track 031

★We're in big trouble.

我們麻煩大了！

深入分析

當你面臨「大麻煩」時，就是一種"big trouble"，表示事情嚴重了、麻煩大了，也就是中文的「事情大條了！」，若是你身陷這種麻煩事，英文就叫做："I'm in big trouble."

實用會話

Ⓐ Let's get out of here.
我們快點閃人吧！

Ⓑ Why? What's wrong?
為什麼？怎麼啦？

Ⓐ Don't you see that? We're in big trouble.
你沒瞧見嗎？我們麻煩大了！

實用會話

Ⓐ Shit.
糟糕！

Ⓑ What?
怎麼啦！

Ⓐ We're in big trouble now.
我們現在麻煩大了！

Ⓑ I'm outta here.
我得趕緊閃人囉！

track 032

★ Don't tell me.

不會吧！

深入分析

"Don't tell me." 的字面意思是「不要告訴我！」，其實這句話是引伸用法，表示發生令人想不到、不敢相信的事時，你就可以說"Don't tell me."，有點類似"I can't believe it."（我真是不敢相信！）

實用會話

Ⓐ I'm not gonna marry Jim.

我不要嫁給吉姆。

Ⓑ Don't tell me.

不會吧！

Ⓐ I won't marry him. I mean it.

我不會和他結婚的！我是說真的！

衍生例句

► Oh, no!

喔！不會吧！

► No way!

不會吧！

track 033

★ No way!

不行！

深入分析

"No way!"字面意思雖然是「沒有方法」、「沒有道路」，其實是指針對對方提出的要求，表達你「不答應」的立場。

前面也提過，若要表示訝異的情境，也可以說"No way!"，表示中文的「不會吧！」、「不可能吧！」、「不可置信」的驚訝用語。

實用會話

A Can I go camping with Jim?

我可以和吉姆去露營嗎？

B No way!

不行！

A Please?

拜託啦！

實用會話

A Check this out.

你來看看！

B No way! I can't believe it.

不會吧！我真不敢相信！

track 034

★Are you joking?

你是開玩笑的吧！

深入分析

要表示對於所聽聞的事感到不敢相信、不置可否時，中文常會說：「你是開玩笑的吧！」英文就可以說："Are you joking?"，若是讓你訝異到說不出話的程度時，你也可以直接說：「不會吧！」，英文就可以說："No way!"

實用會話

A I'm gonna ask Karen out.

我要約凱倫出去！

B Are you joking?

你是開玩笑的吧！

實用會話

A We've decided to get marry tomorrow.

我們已經決定明天要結婚！

B You what? Are you joking?

什麼？你是開玩笑的吧！

衍生例句

► Are you kidding?

你在開玩笑嗎？

► Is it a joke?

這是開玩笑嗎？

▶ No kidding?

不是開玩笑吧？

▶ Are you kidding me?

你在開我玩笑吧？

track 035

★ Don't give me that!

少來這套！

深入分析

若是你對對方的態度或行為不滿意，你就可以說："Don't give me that!"，意思是「你少來了，我不吃你這一套！」除此之外，也表示你不認同、不欣賞或是不相信的意思！

實用會話

Ⓐ Feel better?

好點了嗎？

Ⓑ It hurts.

很痛耶！

Ⓐ Don't give me that!

少來這套！

實用會話

Ⓐ I stayed at home all day.

我一整天都在家裡！

B Don't give me that! I saw you with him.

少來了！我看見你和他在一起！

track 036

★ Are you busy tonight?

你今天晚上忙嗎？

深入分析

當你打算提出邀請時，應該先問問對方是否有空："Are you busy?"意思是「你今天忙嗎？」，句尾的時間副詞可以再加"tonight"、"now"、"tomorrow"等，例如："Are you busy now?"(你現在忙嗎？)

實用會話

A Look, are you busy tonight?

聽好，你今天晚上忙嗎？

B No, why?

不會啊，為什麼這麼問？

A Would you like to go to a party with me?

要不要和我一起去參加派對？

B Yes, I'd love to.

好啊！我想去！

衍生例句

► Will you be free tomorrow evening?

你明晚有空嗎？

track 037

★Are you free on Sunday night?

你星期天晚上有空嗎？

深入分析

"free"表示「自由的」，而常見的"be free"則是「有空閒的」，表示「時間是自由的」，意即「有空閒」、「沒有任何計畫」的意思，所以當你要問某人「現在是否有空」時，就可以問："Are you free now?"

實用會話

A Are you free on Sunday night?
你星期天晚上有空嗎？

B I'm not sure. What's up?
我不確定！有事嗎？

實用會話

A Are you free on Friday night?
你星期五晚上有空嗎？

B I might not be in town. A friend invited me to visit him in Seattle.
我可能不在城裡。有一位朋友邀請我去西雅圖找他。

A Some of us are getting together, and I thought you might want to come too.
我們有一些人要聚會，我想說你可能也會想來！

track 038

★ How about going to a movie?

去看場電影怎麼樣？

深入分析

若要邀約朋友，除了可以問："Will you be free?"（你有空嗎？），也可以直接告訴對方你的提議："How about..."，例如："How about going to a movie?"（要不要一起去看場電影？）

實用會話

Ⓐ Busy now?
現在忙嗎？

Ⓑ Nope.
不會啊！

Ⓐ How about going to a movie?
去看場電影怎麼樣？

Ⓑ I don't think so. I don't want to go out right now.
不要！我現在不想出去！

徹底學會英文

"How about..."是個非常實用的提議句型，可以在about後面加上名詞或動名詞的邀約提議。

➲ How about a drink tonight?
今晚去喝一杯怎樣？

➲ How about this Friday?
要不要就這個星期五？

track 039

★ Somebody's knocking at the door.

有人在敲門！

深入分析

「門外有人在敲門」該怎麼說？很簡單的一句英文，就叫做"Somebody's knocking at the door."，你可能會問：「明明就是『門外』，為什麼叫做"at the door"」，別懷疑，這是英文的慣用語句，記住這麼說就對了！

此外，若是你要問敲門者的身份，中文就會說：「是誰啊！」，英文千萬不能說"Who are you?"，而要問："Who is it?"，門外的人不論男女，主詞都用"it"表示就可以了！

實用會話

A Somebody's knocking at the door.

有人在敲門！

B Who is it?

是誰啊？

C It's me Jack.

是我，傑克。

衍生例句

► Someone is ringing the bell.

有人在按門鈴。

► Someone is at the door.

門外有人！

track 040

★Make yourself at home.

不要拘束！

深入分析

當朋友來訪時，你一定會說「不要拘束」，若要照字面翻譯成英文，絕對是很困難的一件事，但是語言之間的轉換翻譯，應該是以原文的主旨精髓為主，因此英文的對應用法就是："Make yourself at home."，字面意思是「讓你自己在家裡」，也就是中文的「不要拘束」的意思。

實用會話

A Sit down, please.
請坐！

B Thanks!
謝謝！

A Make yourself at home, OK?
不要拘束，好嗎？

B Sure, Mrs. Smith.
好的，史密斯太太。

track 041

★Take a seat, please.

請隨便坐吧！

深入分析

邀請對方「坐下」的語句很簡單，和中文很類似，就是"Take a seat."，中文解釋為「拿一個座位」，也就是「請坐」的意思，至於坐哪裡？就主隨客便囉！

此外，中文「坐下」的英文叫做"sit down"，若要有禮貌地邀請對方坐下，則可以說"Sit down, please."（請坐下）

實用會話

A Hi, Mrs. Smith. It's me, Carol.
嗨，史密斯太太，是我，卡蘿。

B Come on in. Take a seat, please.
進來吧！請隨便坐吧！

A Thank you.
謝謝妳！

B What would you like to drink?
妳想喝點什麼？

實用會話

A I need to talk to you, Mr. Smith.
史密斯先生，我要和你談一談！

B Sit down, please.
請坐吧！

track 042

★Let's go!

走吧！

深入分析

當你準備要動身出發時，可能得先邀約同行者「我們可以走了！」，也就是中文口語中常說的：「我們走吧！」，英文的說法就更簡單，就叫做" Let's go!"

實用會話

A Wait! Let me finish it.

等一下，讓我先做完！

B Hello? I'm in a hurry!

喂！我在趕時間！

A I'm ready. Let's go!

我好了！走吧！

實用會話

A Are you ready?

準備好了嗎？

B Yes.

好了！

A OK. Come on, let's go.

好吧！快點，我們走吧！

徹底學會英文

Shall we?

可以走了嗎？

若是要問對方「要出發了嗎？」、「要出門了嗎？」就可以問對方："Shall we?"，表示「好了嗎？可以出發了吧！」

A：Shall we?

可以走了嗎？

B：No, I'm not ready.

不行，我還沒準備好！

track 043

★ See you.

再見！

深入分析

聽見外國朋友說"See you."可別直楞楞地盯著對方瞧，外國朋友是在和你「道別」的意思。

關於「說再見」這檔子事，中文有：「再見！」或是年輕人間常用的「閃人囉！」，還有外來語用法的「拜拜！」英文的說法種類也不遑多讓，最常見的就是"Good-bye."、"Bye."

實用會話

A It's nice talking to you.

和你談話很愉快！

B Me too.

我也是！

A See you.

再見！

B Bye.

再見！

衍生例句

► Good-bye.

= Bye.

= See you later.

= See you soon.

再見！

track 044

★ Talk to you later.

再聊囉！

深入分析

中文的對話之間，若說「再聊囉！」，有兩種意思，一種是「我不想說」，另一種則是「我要準備說再見」的意思，通常可以從談話內容或對話時間的長短來判斷對方的意思，若是很長時間的聊天後，對方說「再聊囉！」，也就是暗示你「要說再見」的意思，英文的用法也是相同，就叫做"Talk to you later."

實用會話

A It's getting late now.

時間很晚了！

B Yeah, it is.

是啊！是很晚了！

A Talk to you later.

再聊囉！

B Sure. Bye.

好啊！再見！

實用會話

A Well, all right, I'll talk to you later. You take care and be safe.

好吧，就這樣囉！再見！你要保重，小心一點！

B I will. Bye-bye.

我會的，再見！

track 045

★ Let's keep in touch.

要保持聯絡喔！

深入分析

遇見久違不見的朋友時，在互相道別時，你一定會說：「要保持聯絡喔！」，這句話的英文就叫做"Let's keep in touch."（讓我們保持聯絡）。"keep in touch"是常用片語，字面意思是「保持相互接觸」，也就是「保持聯絡」的意思。

實用會話

Ⓐ Nice talking to you. See you soon.

和你談話很愉快！再見。

Ⓑ Let's keep in touch. Bye.

要保持聯絡喔！再見

實用會話

Ⓐ Do you still keep in touch with anyone from school?

你有和學校的同學保持聯絡嗎？

Ⓑ Yes, Maggie and David. How about you?

有啊，瑪姬和大衛！你呢？

Ⓐ No, I don't. I just came back from Seattle last week.

沒有，我沒有！我上個星期才剛從西雅圖回來！

徹底學會英文

Don't be a stranger!

要多多聯絡喔！

若是可能確知彼此會有一段時間不再見面，要在臨道別前希望彼此能「保持聯絡」，卻又不想要直接說"keep in touch"時，就可以說 "Don't be a stranger."，字面意思是指「不要變成陌生人」，也就是希望彼此要「多保持聯絡，以免變成陌生人」的意思，例如同事可能要離職、鄰居要搬離開等情境都適用。

此外，好友要結婚了，你也可以說："Don't be a stranger!"，這是一句玩笑話，表示「不要見色忘友，因為結婚而減少和朋友的聯絡」的提醒用語！

又例如，你可以對那種很少和大家聯絡的人，直接稱呼："Stranger."，表示「大家都快要不認識你了！」

A：What a nice visit. I look forward to seeing you next time.
　真高興來訪！我好期待下次再來拜訪！

B：Yeah, don't be a stranger!
　是啊，要多多聯絡喔！

A：See you later.
　再見！

B：OK, but don't be a stranger.
　再見，要多多聯絡喔！

track 046

★I'll see you at six.

六點鐘見。

深入分析

若是你和人有約定在未來的某個時間點彼此要再見面，在臨道別的時候，你就可以說："I'll see you at＋數字"，表示雙方「要在幾點鐘見面」的意思，也可以具有順便和對方確認，再見面的時間點是否正確！

實用會話

Ⓐ Where do you want to meet?
你想在哪裡見面？

B In my office.

在我的辦公室！

A OK! There comes my bus. Bye.

好！我的公車來了。再見囉！

B Sure. I'll see you at six.

好！六點鐘見囉！

A OK. See you.

好啊！再見。

track 047

★ Says who?

誰說的？

深入分析

若是你不認同對方的意見、質疑對方所說的事，中文就會說：「誰說的？」或是「才不是呢！」，這樣的意思英文要怎麼說呢？非常簡單，就叫做：" Says who?"，表示「是誰說的？」此外，還可以解釋為「誰是老大？」或是「誰說了算？」的質疑用法。

實用會話

A It is Jack. I'm so sure.

是傑克！我很確定！

B Says who?

誰說（是傑克）的？

A Who but Jack would do such a thing?

除了傑克，還有誰會做這種事呢？

實用會話

A Maybe we should change our plans.

也許我們應該要改變我們的計畫！

B Says who?

誰說應該要的？

衍生例句

▶ Who told you that?

誰告訴你的？

track 048

★What's your plan?

你的計畫是什麼？

深入分析

當一群人同意要參加一個活動或進行一件事時，準備要付諸行動之前，你就可以問問主事者："What's your plan?"，字面意思是「你的計畫是什麼？」也就是暗示對方「說來聽聽」的意思。

實用會話

A I can't wait to see him.

我等不及要見他了！

B What's your plan?

你的計畫是什麼？

A Listen, maybe we can give him a surprise.

聽好，也許我們可以給他一個驚喜！

徹底學會英文

What's your plan B?

你的替代方案是什麼？

「如果這個計畫失敗，那是不是有替代方案呢？」這樣長的一句中文，要用英文表達肯定很難吧？一點都不會，只要說："What's your plan B?"就可以啦！

A：What do you think?

你覺得呢？

B：Well, I don't know. What's your plan B?

嗯…，我不知道耶！你的B計畫是什麼？

track 049

★Why not?

好呀！

深入分析

一般說來，「答應」或「認同」的回答通常是用"yes"表示，但是中文也常常說「有何不可？」，英文中也有相對應的說法，就叫做"Why not?"，雖然是疑問句型，卻可以表示「好啊！」、「有何不可」的意思。

實用會話

A Will you pick me up at my place?

你會到我的住處來接我嗎？

B Sure. Why not?

好呀！有何不可！

實用會話

A Maybe we should try to figure it out.

也許我們應該試試理出個頭緒。

B Sure. Why not?

好呀！有何不可！

track 050

★Why not?

為什麼不？

深入分析

當對方說了一句否定語句，但是你不知道他為什麼會持這個否定的立場時，你就可以先反問對方："Why not?"，例如兒子不想去上學時，你就可以問："Why not?"，這是一句你想要追究原因的反問句。

實用會話

A How do you like New York?

你喜歡紐約嗎？

B I'm not used to the city yet.

我還不習慣都市生活！

A Why not?

為什麼不習慣？

B You know why.

你知道原因啊！

track 051

★ No problem!

沒問題！

深入分析

當對方問了你一個「能否…」的問題，若是你的回答是"Yes."，那麼你也可以用"No problem!"表示，有點類似中文的「沒問題！」或是「包在我身上」的意思。

此外，若是對方是向你說謝謝，你的回應除了"You're welcome."之外，也可以說："No problem!"，表示「不客氣」的意思。

實用會話

A Can you send this letter for me?

可以幫我寄這封信嗎？

B No problem! I'll do it on my way home.

沒問題！我會在回家的路上去寄。

實用會話

A Thank you for your help.

謝謝你的幫忙！

B No problem!

不客氣！

track 052

★What were you thinking?

你搞什麼鬼？

深入分析

當對方做了一件令人覺得不可思議的事時，你一定會很生氣地問：「你搞什麼鬼？」英文要怎麼說？可是和「鬼」一點關係都沒有喔，你可以說："What were you thinking?"，字面意思是「你在想什麼？」，也就是因為不知對方是怎麼盤算的，所以帶有「你搞什麼鬼？」的質問意味。

實用會話

A Take a look at this.

你來看這個東西！

B What? What were you thinking?

什麼東西？你搞什麼鬼？

A Don't you think this is beautiful?

你不覺得這個很漂亮嗎？

B No, I don't think so.

不，我不覺得！

衍生例句

▶ What happened to you?

你怎麼了？

track 053

★ What's your problem?

你腦袋有問題啊！

深入分析

不同的語氣會製造出不同的解釋，以"What's your problem?"為例，雖然字面意思是「你的問題是什麼？」，但若是在雙方爭執、意見不同的情境下，則有質疑對方「你的腦袋有問題」的意思。

實用會話

A He's such a chicken.

他真是個膽小鬼。

B What's your problem? What you said was not quite true.

你腦袋有問題啊！你所說的完全不符合事實。

實用會話

A You're driving me crazy.

你快把我弄瘋了！

B What's your problem?

你腦袋有問題啊！

C Please, guys, just listen to me.

拜託，各位，聽我說！

衍生例句

► What's wrong with you?

你哪根筋不對勁？

track 054

★ Shit.

糟糕！

深入分析

外國人老是將"Shit."掛在嘴邊，不明究理的人還以為他們老是拿「排泄物」在發洩吧！其實"Shit."的確是一種短而強烈的情緒抒發用語，但是中文可以對應的解釋非常多，可以解釋為「糟糕」、「慘了」、「見鬼」…等等，可以依照當時的情境來解釋翻譯的用語喔！

實用會話

A Shit.

糟糕！

B What?

怎麼啦！

A We're in big trouble now.

我們現在麻煩大了！

衍生例句

▶ My God.

天啊！

▶ What?

什麼？

▶ I can't believe it.

真是不敢相信！

track 055

★ What should I do?

我該怎麼辦？

深入分析

當你急得像熱鍋上的螞蟻般手足無措，實在不知道該怎麼辦，就可以說："What should I do?"，有求助旁人給予你意見的意味。

實用會話

A I don't know what to do.

我不知道該怎麼辦！

B Just calm down.

先冷靜下來！

A What should I do?

我該怎麼辦？

實用會話

A My God! What should I do now?

天哪！我現在該怎麼辦？

B Come on, just take a break.

不要這樣，就先休息一下吧！

衍生例句

► I have no idea.

我一點想法都沒有！

► I don't know what to do.

我不知道該怎麼做！

track 056

★ Gee.

天啊！

深入分析

和"My God."（我的老天！）用法有一點類似，是屬於驚嘆語句，中文的翻譯可以是「老天爺！」、「唉喔！」等意思，都是屬於在令人不敢相信、訝異的情境中使用。

實用會話

A Hello?

喂？

B David? This is Carol.

大衛嗎？我是卡蘿！

A Gee, I'm so glad you called!

唉呀！真高興妳打電話過來！

B Do you have any plans tonight?

你今天晚上有事嗎？

A No. Why?

沒事啊！怎麼啦？

實用會話

A Gee, it's been a long time.

天啊！好久了喔！

B You've not changed at all.

你一點都沒變！

實用會話

A Be careful, young lady.

小姐，小心喔！

B Gee, thanks.

天啊！多謝啦！

track 057

★ Talk to him.

你勸勸他。

深入分析

中文「勸」在英文的說法有"advise"、"persuade"等，但若是「你勸勸他」、「你開導開導他」這種和對方「談一談」的情境，則只要簡單地說："Talk to him."，是一種祇使句的用語，所以talk前面不加"to"，也不改為"talking"。

若勸說的對象是女性，則受詞"him"應該改為："her"，或是直接加人名，例如："Talk to Jim."（你勸勸吉姆）

實用會話

A Talk to him.

你勸勸他。

B Come on, he is your responsibility.

拜託，他是你的責任耶！

A Me? I don't think so.

我？我才不要！

track 058

★ Are you happy now?

你現在滿意了吧？

深入分析

語言的奧妙就在於你聽到的未必是對方真正要表達的意思，例如我們可能會問：「你現在滿意了吧？」，意思就是說「這下子你稱心如意了吧！」可是事實上，帶有一點「我不爽」的意思，無巧不巧，英文也有相對應的用法："Are you happy now?"，是不是和中文簡直就像雙胞胎的語法與意思呢？

實用會話

A Are you happy now?
你現在滿意了吧？

B Yeah, why not?
是啊！怎會不高興呢！

A Fine.
隨便你！

實用會話

A Are you happy now?
你現在滿意了吧？

B Hey, don't talk to me like that.
嘿，別這樣子和我說話！

track 059

★ I'll be right back.

我會馬上回來！

深入分析

當你需要告訴對方：「我會馬上回來！」時，英文怎麼說？首先要知道「回來」的英文慣用法為"be back"，所以「我會回來」就叫做"I'll be back."，而"right"為「馬上」、「立即」的副詞，所以「我會馬上回來！」就叫做"I'll be right back."

實用會話

A Daddy, get me out of here.
爹地，救我出去！

B Stay where you are. I'll be right back.
不要亂跑！我會馬上回來！

A Hurry up.
快一點！

衍生例句

▶ I'll be back right away.
= I'll be back immediately.
= I'll be back at once.
我會馬上回來！

track 060

★I'll be with you in an instant.

我立刻就來。

深入分析

和前面的"I'll be right back."（我會馬上回來！）不太一樣，特別強調的是「我會回到你身邊」的意思，可能是回來服務、提供所需物品等，但是一般的狀況下，二者的說法是可以互通的。

"in an instant"和"right away"或是"right now"類似，都是「立即」、「立刻」…等，表示「不用一會兒功夫的時間」。

實用會話

A May I have a glass of water?
能給我一杯水嗎？

B Yes, I'll be with you in an instant.
好的！我立刻就來。

實用會話

A Carol? Where are you? I can't find my glasses.
卡蘿？妳在哪裡？我找不到我的眼鏡！

B OK, I'll be with you in an instant.
好！我立刻就來。

track 061

★Think fast.

快點做決定！

深入分析

若是對方對某件事遲遲無法做出決定，你就可以催促對方：「快點決定！」英文就叫做"Think fast."，字面意思是「想快一點」，但意思就是催促對方「好好想想、做出決定」的意思，是帶有祈使句的語意。

實用會話

A Think fast. Which do you prefer?
快點做決定。你要哪一個？

B I'll take the blue one.
我會選藍色這一個！

A No problem. I'll be back immediately.
沒問題！我馬上回來！

衍生例句

▶ Make up your mind.
快點下決定！

track 062

★ I'm offering you a deal.

我提供你一個交易。

深入分析

"offer someone a deal" 表示「提供交易給某人」，通常是要讓對方思考如何選擇或做出決定的意思。

實用會話

A I'm offering you a deal.

我提供你一個交易。

B What kind of deal?

什麼交易？

A Here you are.

這個！

B Oh, this is really important for me.

喔！這對我來說真的很重要！

實用會話

A I need to get the rest of the hospital bill paid.

我需要付清醫院的帳單！

B Good. Now I'm offering you a deal.

很好！現在我提供你一個交易。

衍生例句

▶ Do you want this deal?

你想要接受這個交易嗎？

track 063

★ That's not fair.

不公平！

深入分析

「人生從來就不會是公平」，但是當你面對「不公平」的事件時，仍然可以發出你的「不平之鳴」，英文就叫做："That's not fair."，"fair" 表示「公平的」，而若是要表達「對某人不公平」，則可以說："It's not fair to someone."

實用會話

A Here you are.

這個給你！

B That's not fair. I don't want it.

不公平！我不要這個！

A Nobody said life was fair.

沒有人說人生是公平的啊！

衍生例句

▶ It's not fair.

不公平！

track 064

★I can't hear you.

我聽不見你說話！

深入分析

語言之間轉換的有趣之處，就在於不必逐字翻譯，例如：「我聽不見你說話！」，在英文中只要說："I can't hear you."，字面意思表示「我聽不見你」，也就是「我聽不見你所說的話」，但是「說話」兩個字卻不必翻譯出來，例如在和對方對話、電話中…等，不管是收訊不好、線路有雜音等等的情境中都適用。

實用會話

A Sam, I can't hear you. Hello?
山姆？我聽不見你說話！喂？

B Hello? Sandy? Don't hang up!
喂？珊蒂？不要掛斷電話！

實用會話

A Jim? Can you hear me?
吉姆？你聽得到我說話嗎？

B Who is this? Hello?
你是誰？喂？

A I can't hear you. Are you there?
我聽不見你說話！你還在嗎？

track 065

★Did you hear me?

你有聽到嗎？

深入分析

當你說了一堆話後，對方仍像是丈二金剛般摸不著頭緒，你就可以說："Did you hear me?"，通常用過去式的疑問句表示，是因為要確認「我剛剛說的話你有聽見嗎？」

實用會話

A Did you hear me?

你有聽到嗎？

B Sorry?

抱歉？

A I said don't forget to hand in your paper tomorrow.

我説不要忘記明天要交你的報告。

B But I'm gonna...

可是我要去…

A You heard me.

你有聽到我説的話了吧！

track 066

★You heard me.

你聽到我說的話了！

深入分析

當對方老是問你同樣的問題時，你就會說：「你有聽到我說的話了！」，英文就可以說："You heard me."，表示「不要再問了！」或「我已經說過了，你也聽到了！」的意思。此外，若是對方質疑你所下的命令，你也可以說："You heard me."表示「我說了算，你有聽見吧！」

實用會話

A Why should I obey the rules?

為什麼我要遵守規定！

B You heard me.

你有聽到我說的話了！

A OK! Give me five more minutes.

好吧！再多給我五分鐘的時間！

實用會話

A You heard me, didn't you? Maybe you should...

你有聽到我說的話了，對吧？也許你應該…

B I did. Say no more, please.

我有聽到！拜託別再說了！

A Oh, good.

喔，好吧！

track 067

★ Hello!

哈囉！

深入分析

你一定也常聽見外國人說"Hello!"吧？除了表示中文「你好」的打招呼之外，也可以是發出聲音提醒對方注意，或是試探性詢問這個地方是否有人在的意思，類似中文的電話用語的「喂」，或是口語中的「請問一下」、「有人在嗎？」、「聽我說話」…等多種情境。

實用會話

A Hello, David.

哈囉，大衛。

B Hi, Sandy, I haven't seen you for months.

嗨，珊蒂，好幾個月不見了！

實用會話

A Hello?

喂？

B Karen?

凱倫？

A Who is speaking?

你是哪一位？

B This is Chuck.

我是查克。

A Oh, hi, Chuck, what's up?

喔，嗨，查克，有事嗎？

實用會話

A Hello! I am here.

喂！我人還在這裡耶！

B Oh, sorry, we didn't see you.

喔，抱歉，我們沒看到你！

C Why are you still here?

你為什麼在這裡？

實用會話

A Hello?

有人在嗎？

B What the hell are you doing here?

你在這裡做搞什麼？

A Nothing. I am just... you know.

沒事啊！我只是…你知道的啦！

B Hey, how did you get in here?

對了！你怎麼進來這裡的？

實用會話

A Hello?

有人嗎？

B Over here.

在這裡！

A Oh, here you are. What were you doing here?

喔，你在這裡喔！你在這裡做什麼？

track 068

★Hello, you guys.

哈囉，大家好。

深入分析

若是要打招呼的對象不只一人，而是一群不分男女老幼的對象時，就可以說："Hello, you guys."，表示「你們大家好」的意思。

"hello"的後面接打招呼的對象名詞，例如若是打招呼對象是年輕女性，則可以說"Hello, girls."，表示「各位女孩妳們好！」

實用會話

A Hello, you guys.

哈囉，大家好！

B Hey, it's so good see you again.

嘿，真高興又看到你。

C You look so different.

你看起來不太一樣喔！

實用會話

A Hello, everyone.

哈囉！各位。

B Chuck! Where have you been?

查克！你到哪兒去了？

C We really worry about you.

我們真的很擔心你耶！

A I'm OK. Don't worry about me.

我很好！別擔心我！

衍生例句

- Hello, everyone.

  各位，你們好！

- Hello, ladies and gentlemen.

  各位女士、各位先生，你們好！

- Hello, kids.

  小朋友們，你們好！

track 069

★ Please.

拜託啦！

深入分析

中文常見的請求語句是「拜託啦！」，英文的相對應的說法就叫做"Please."，表示是「請求」的意思，可以使用疑問句及祈求句的語氣。

實用會話

A Can I go fishing with Dad?

我能和爸爸去釣魚嗎？

B We'll see.

再說吧！

A Please?

拜託啦！

B You heard me.

你聽見我說的話了！（別再說了！）

實用會話

A Please. This is really important for my family.

拜託，這對我家人來說真的很重要！

B OK! I'll see what I can do.

好吧！我來想辦法！

track 070

★I wasn't expecting you so soon.

沒想到你會這麼早到！

深入分析

當有人要在某個時間來訪時，你一定會預期（expect）對方到達的時間，若是對方提早到達、或是比你預期的時間還早時，就可以說："I wasn't expecting you so soon."

實用會話

Ⓐ Hi, I'm from CNS, the computer company.
嗨，我是CNS電腦公司的人。

Ⓑ Oh, I wasn't expecting you so soon.
喔，沒想到你會這麼早到！

實用會話

Ⓐ I wasn't expecting you so soon.
沒想到你會這麼早到！

Ⓑ Should I come back later?
我應該稍後再來嗎？

Ⓐ How about 10:30?
十點半可以嗎？

Ⓑ Sure. Why not?
好啊！有何不可！

track 071

★ Yeah, for now.

是啊，目前為止是的！

深入分析

當對方提出一個是非的問題，而答案正好符合你目前的情況，但是將來的狀況，卻不是你之後可以預期的，此時你就可以說："Yeah, for now."，表示「目前為止的確是如此的！」

若情況是相反的，則只要說："Nope, not for now."

實用會話

A Are you alone?

你自己一個人嗎？

B Yeah, for now.

是啊，目前為止是的！

A I see.

我瞭解了！

實用會話

A Did you work on it?

你有在忙這件事嗎？

B Nope, not for now.

沒有，目前為止沒有！

track 072

★I'm Maria.

我叫做瑪麗亞。

深入分析

當你要向對方自我介紹時，中文就說：「我叫做…」，英文的說法就更簡單，直接說："I'm..."就直接有「我的名字叫做…」的意思。

實用會話

A Hi, my name is Carol.

嗨，我叫做卡蘿。

B I'm Maria. I take care of this building.

我叫做瑪麗亞，我負責這棟建築物！

實用會話

A This way, please, Mr. Smith.

史密斯先生，這邊請。

B No, call me Jim, please.

不要這樣，稱呼我吉姆就好！

A OK, Jim.

好吧，吉姆！

衍生例句

► Just call me Maria.

請稱呼我瑪莉亞就好！

► My name is Maria.

我的名字是瑪麗亞。

track 073

★ Ah, good.

喔，好吧！

深入分析

"Ah, good."的解釋很微妙，可以使用在回覆所說的話，帶有一點贊同、瞭解的意思，沒有多大的意思，也可以是單純地當作回應對方所說的話的一種附和用語，也可以解釋為中文的「是這樣喔，好吧！」的意思。

實用會話

A Did he tell you the nearest hotel is 50 miles away?

他有告訴過你最近的飯店在50英哩遠嗎？

B Yeah, but it might be easier if I just stay here.

有啊！但是我住在這裡會比較方便。

A Ah, good.

喔，好吧！

track 074

★Where were you?

你跑去哪裡了？

深入分析

當你找不到某人，而對方卻又突然出現時，你就可問問對方「你跑去哪裡了？」英文就叫做：" Where were you?"，通常會用過去式的句型表達，表示「我之前有在找你，你當時在哪裡」的意思。此外，也可以在句尾加註時間，以說明當時找人的時間。

實用會話

Ⓐ Where were you?
你跑去哪裡了？

Ⓑ Just playing with the dog. Don't worry.
我只是和狗在玩，不用擔心！

實用會話

Ⓐ Where were you, sweetie?
小甜心，妳去哪裡了？

Ⓑ I went to see a movie with Eric.
我和艾瑞克去看電影！

實用會話

Ⓐ Where were you last night?
你昨天晚上去哪裡了？

B I went shopping with my friends.

我和朋友去逛街！

徹底學會英文

Where have you been?

這陣子你都到哪兒去了？

同樣都是問「你人到哪兒去了？」的問句，但是兩種問句各自有不同的詢問目的。

以"Where were you?"來說，多半是指過去的某一時段時間，你「人在哪裡」或「做了什麼事」。

而"Where have you been?"則是指兩人因為好長一段時間未曾見面，如今兩人再見時，主要是想知道：「這一段時間以來，你人都在哪裡？是否發生了什麼我不知道的事？」

A：Hi, Eric!
嗨，艾瑞克！

B：Sandy! Long time no see.
珊蒂！好久不見！

A：Yeah, it's been a while.
是啊！有好長一段時間了！

B：Where have you been?
這陣子妳都到哪兒去了？

A：I went back home for Christmas.
我回家去過聖誕節！

track 075

★ Already?

已經到了？

深入分析

當某件事已經發生，而這件事也是你早就預期會發生，當你由對方口中證實的確發生時，就可以用訝異的口吻說："Already?"，表示「已經…」的意思。

實用會話

A This is the lady we were expecting.
這位女士就是我們在等的人！

B Already?
（她）已經到了？

實用會話

A Jim's arrived in New York.
吉姆已經到紐約了！

B Already? Did you meet him at the airport?
已經到了？你有去機場接機嗎？

A Nope. Why?
沒有啊！為什麼這麼問？

track 076

★ Sure, right this way.

好的！這邊請！

深入分析

當你需要為某人領路、帶位時，中文就會說：「這邊請！」，英文就叫做"This way."，字面的意思是「這個方向」，也就是順著妳所指引的方向走的用意。正式一點的說法則為："This way, please."（請走這邊）

實用會話

A Why don't you show her around and set her up in room 502.

你何不帶她到處逛一逛，然後把她安頓在502號房。

B Sure, right this way.

好的！這邊請！

衍生例句

▶ This way, please.

這邊請！

▶ Follow me.

跟我來！

▶ Come with me.

一起來吧！

track 077

★ Be polite.

要有禮貌！

深入分析

若是要告誡對方「要有禮貌」，通常是使用「祈使句型」，也就是動詞在句首："Be polite."。"be"在這句話中是表示「成為…」的意思，而"polite"是形容詞「有禮貌的」，整句話也就是「要遵守禮貌行為的約束」。

實用會話

A Come on, let's go.

快點，我們走吧！

B OK, Mr. Parker.

好啊！派克先生！

C Be polite, kid.

小朋友，要有禮貌！

B I will, mom.

我會的，媽咪！

track 078

★Do you smoke?

你有抽菸嗎？

深入分析

要問對方「有沒有抽菸」就可以直接問："Do you smoke?"，和中文一樣簡單的問句，實用又好記，又不用任何片語，類似簡單問句還有「你喝酒嗎？」，就可以說："Do you drink?"

實用會話

A Do you smoke?

你有抽菸嗎？

B Well, sometimes.

嗯，有時候（有抽菸）！

A No smoking in the building. They are the rules.

在這棟建築物內不准抽菸。這是規定！

B This is great.

真是太好！（反諷用法）

track 079

★Here is your room.

這是你的房間！

深入分析

帶領人到他所住的地方時，就可以說"Here is your room."，例如當飯店的服務生帶領客人到房間內時，就會說："Here is your room."，意思是「這是您的房間」。若是對方仍一直站在房間內沒有離去時，就表示他正在等你的小費，千萬不要忘記給小費（tip）喔！

實用會話

A Here is your room.

這是你的房間！

B This place is pretty good shape.

這裡非常井然有序！

A Yeah, mom likes to keep everything spotless.

是啊！媽媽喜歡乾乾淨淨的。

衍生例句

▶ Here it is.

就是這裡啦！

track 080

★This is impressive.

這真是令人印象深刻！

深入分析

若是某件事「令人印象深刻」，請記住這句英文用法："This is impressive."，不但表示你的「印象深刻」，也帶有一點「讚美」的意味，表示「很難忘」的意思。此外，你也可以簡單地說："Impressive."

實用會話

A Look over here.

看這裡！

B OK. This is impressive.

很好！這真是令人印象深刻。

實用會話

A What do you think of my idea?

你覺得我的主意如何？

B I think it's impressive.

我覺得令人印象深刻！

衍生例句

▶ This is amazing.

真是令人訝異啊！

▶ Unbelievable.

真是令人不敢相信！

track 081

★This is great.

太好了！

深入分析

適時的「讚美」是一種良好人際互動，若是對方因為表現得好，你可以說"Well done."或"Good job."，若是你認同對方提出的主意，則可以說 "Good idea."，在這兩者之外的情境下，舉凡是你要表達「這個結果很好」「這個狀況令人感到放心、滿意」等，都可以簡單地說："This is great."，表示「很好」、「不錯」的意思。

實用會話

Ⓐ I'm gonna make up with her.

我要去補償她。

Ⓑ This is great.

太好了！

實用會話

Ⓐ Check this out. What do you think of it?

你看！你的看法如何？

Ⓑ This is great for you.

這對你來說太好了！

track 082

★ Congratulations.

恭喜！

深入分析

若是要表示「道賀」、「恭喜」，就非常適合說"Congratulations."。要注意，一定要使用複數形式表示，代表「很多恭喜」的意思，千萬不能只是說："Congratulation."

實用會話

A Maria? Long time no see. How have you been?

瑪麗亞？好久不見！妳好嗎？

B Good. I just got married last week.

很好！我上週結婚了！

A Congratulations.

恭喜！

實用會話

A You know what? I passed my final exam.

你知道嗎？我的期末考及格了！

B Congratulations. We're so proud of you.

恭喜！我們以你為榮！

衍生例句

▶ Good for you.

對你來說是好事！

▶ Good to hear that.

很高興知道這件事！

▶ I'm so happy for you.

我真是為你感到高興！

track 083

★ Sucks.

糟透了！

深入分析

"Sucks."是非常口語化的用語，表示「糟透了」、「不好」的意思，可以指人、事、物等，例如有人問你這部電影好不好看，若是「爛透了」，你就可以說："It sucks."，最好在同輩之間使用，不要在長輩或正式場合中使用。

實用會話

Ⓐ What do you think of this movie?

你覺得這部電影好看嗎？

Ⓑ Sucks.

糟透了！

實用會話

A So?

所以呢？

B It sucks. Everything sucks.

爛透了！每件事都爛透了！

A Are you OK?

你還好吧？

衍生例句

► It's terrible.

糟透了！

track 084

★ You're telling me.

還用你說！

深入分析

當你嫌對方很囉唆或是要制止對方繼續嘮叨時，你可以說："You're telling me."，這句話可不是「你在告訴我」的意思，而是表示「還用你說，我都知道」的意思，表示「我早就知道了」。

實用會話

A Why don't you stop drinking?

你何不戒煙？

Ⓑ You're telling me.

還用你說！

實用會話

Ⓐ Jim's in a really bad mood today.

吉姆今天心情很差！

Ⓑ You're telling me!

還用你說！

track 085

★ She's kind of crazy.

她有點瘋狂。

深入分析

"be kind of"表示「有一點」、「稍微」的意思。類似的用法還有"sort of"。

實用會話

Ⓐ What do you think of Carol?

你覺得卡蘿怎麼樣？

Ⓑ Carol? Well, she's kind of crazy.

卡蘿？嗯，她有點瘋狂。

Ⓐ Yeah, I think so, too.

是啊，我也這麼認為！

實用會話

Ⓐ It's kind of cold, isn't it?

有點冷，對吧！

B Yeap. It's chilly.

是啊！冷斃了！

A By the way, I'm Jim.

對了，我叫做吉姆。

實用會話

A I felt I'd met her somewhere before.

我覺得我以前在哪裡有見過她。

B Well..., it's sort of strange.

是喔，有點奇怪喔！

track 086

★ You're afraid of darkness, aren't you?

你很怕黑，對嗎？

深入分析

"be afraid of something"表示「害怕某事或某物」的意思，是一個常見的慣用語句。of後面加所害怕的事，通常是"of＋名詞"或是"of＋形容詞＋名詞"的架構。

實用會話

A Can we get the lights back on?

可以把燈打開嗎？

Ⓑ You're afraid of darkness, aren't you?

你很怕黑，對嗎？

實用會話

Ⓐ I'm afraid of heights.

我有懼高症。

Ⓑ Me, too.

我也是！

---

track 087

★ What's wrong?

怎麼啦？

深入分析

當發現事有蹊蹺或是令人不解時，你就可以問："What's wrong?"，表示你的疑問與不解。

實用會話

Ⓐ The lights go off every 10 minutes.

電燈每十分鐘就會熄滅。

Ⓑ Why? What's wrong?

為什麼？怎麼啦？

實用會話

Ⓐ What's wrong?

怎麼啦？

B Nothing. I thouhght I saw something...

沒事！我以為我看到什麼東西了！

衍生例句

▶ What happened?

發生什麼事了？

▶ Is there something wrong?

有問題嗎？

track 088

★ Home, sweet home.

真是甜蜜的家啊！

深入分析

美國人對家庭的觀念雖然和東方人不太一樣，但不變是對「家」的溫暖感覺，所以英文對家的形容常見"Home, sweet home."，表示「還是家裡溫暖」，說這句話時通常有一種感慨或是惜福的認知，若要套用中文對「家」的形容，有一句俚語很適合：「金窩銀窩，還是自己的狗窩好！」

實用會話

A Here it is.

就是這裡啦！

B Home, sweet home.

真是甜蜜的家啊！

實用會話

Ⓐ Welcome home, baby.

寶貝，歡迎你回家！

Ⓑ Home, sweet home.

還是家裡溫暖！

track 089

★ Sorry?

你說什麼？

深入分析

若是一時之間沒有聽清楚對方所說的話，你可以說："Sorry?"，表示「抱歉，我剛剛沒有聽清楚！」在這裡可不是「對不起」的道歉語句喔！

實用會話

Ⓐ What do you think he'll say?

你覺得他會說什麼？

Ⓑ Sorry?

你說什麼？

Ⓐ I mean do you think he'd get angry?

你覺得他會生氣嗎？

衍生例句

▶ I'm sorry?

你說什麼？

▶ Excuse me?

你說什麼？

▶ Pardon?

再說一遍？

▶ I beg your pardon.

請再說一遍！

track 090

★ It's a long story.

說來話長！

深入分析

若是事情不是三言兩語可以說得清楚的，或是事情不是一時半刻可以解釋清楚的，都叫做「說來話長」，有一種無奈的情緒，英文中文也有一模一樣的用法："It's a long story."，字面意思表示「這是很長的故事」，也就是中文「說來話長」的意思。

實用會話

A What the hell are you doing here?

你在這裡做什麼？

B It's a long story.

說來話長！

Ⓐ Try me.

說來聽聽啊！

track 091

★Let's just say you're right.

也許你是對的！

深入分析

暫時認同對方的論點時，你就可以說："Let's just say you're right."，表示「就當你是對的」。

實用會話

Ⓐ Don't you think it's weird?

你不覺得事情有點詭異？

Ⓑ Let's just say you're right.

也許你是對的！

實用會話

Ⓐ He's so weird.

他真是古怪！

Ⓑ Fine, let's just say you are right.

好吧！就當你是對的！

衍生例句

▶ OK, so, maybe you're right.

好吧，也許你是對的！

track 092

★ You can say that again!

你說的沒錯！

深入分析

認同對方的看法時，你可以說："You can say that again!"，字面意思是「你可以再說一次」，也就是「你說的沒錯，可以再說一次的」意思。

實用會話

A I think Michael Jackson was one of the best singers.

我覺得麥可傑克森是最棒的歌手之一。

B You can say that again!

你說的沒錯！

實用會話

A Let's just say you are right and he is wrong.

就當你是對的，他是錯的！

B You can say that again.

你說的沒錯！

track 093

★Who is in charge here?

誰是這裡的負責人？

深入分析

若是你需要找某人來負責你的客訴或抱怨時，絕對要記得問問對方："Who is in charge here?"，表示你要找那個「最大咖」的負責人來和你協調！

實用會話

A Excuse me.

請問一下！

B Yes?

請說！

A Can you tell me who is in charge here?

你能告訴我誰是這裡的負責人嗎？

B It's Mr. Smith. He's over there.

是史密斯先生！他在那裡！

track 094

★Someone took the key.

有人拿走鑰匙了！

深入分析

若是有某個人做了某件事，「某個人」就可以用"someone"表示，例如「某人打電話給你」，就叫做"someone called you."。

實用會話

A I couldn't find the key. Someone took the key.

我找不到鑰匙。有人拿走鑰匙了！

B What key?

什麼鑰匙？

A The key that opens the front door.

就是打開前門的鑰匙啊！

實用會話

A What can I do for you?

有什麼需要我協助嗎？

B Someone took my bags.

有人拿了我的袋子！

實用會話

A Any messages for me?

有我的留言嗎？

B Someone called you this morning.

今天早上有人打電話給你！

track 095

★Any problem?

有問題嗎？

深入分析

當你發覺對方臉色不對或是氣氛不對時，都可以問對方「有沒有問題？」，英文就叫做"Any problem?"，完整的句子是"Do you have any problem?"

實用會話

Ⓐ Listen, could you come over here?
聽好，你能過來嗎？

Ⓑ Right now?
現在嗎？

Ⓐ Yeah, right now. Any problem?
是啊，就是現在。有問題嗎？

Ⓑ No, no, no... not at all.
沒有，沒有，完全沒有問題！

衍生例句

► Is there something wrong?
有問題嗎？

► What happened?
發生什麼事了？

► Are you OK?
你還好吧？

track 096

★Come over here, please.

請過來這裡！

深入分析

若是你希望對方能向你的方向走過來，中文會說：「請向前走一步！」，在英文中就只要說："Come over here."，是一句原形動詞當句首的祈使句。

實用會話

A Come over here, please.

請過來這裡！

B Come over? What for?

過去？為什麼？

A Is this your bag?

這是你的袋子嗎？

B No, it's not mine.

不是，這不是我的東西！

track 097

★You promise?

你保證？

深入分析

當對方拍胸脯保證、誇下豪語願意承擔時，若是你心存質疑，就可以質疑對方：「你敢保證嗎？」，英文就叫做："You promise?"，表示「我不太相信你說的話耶！」

實用會話

A I'll find her.

我會找到她的。

B You promise?

你保證？

A Yes, I promise.

是的，我保證！

衍生例句

► Are you sure?

你確定嗎？

► No kidding?

不是開玩笑的吧？

track 098

★ I promise.

我保證。

深入分析

當你答應對方，並希望對方能放心你的承諾時，中文的情境是拍拍胸脯說：「我保證！」在英文中則可以說："I promise."

實用會話

A You'll go to the school with me, right?

你會陪我去學校，對嗎？

B I promise.

我保證。

實用會話

A Don't leave me alone.

不要丟下我一個人！

B I promise I won't.

我保證你我不會！

衍生例句

▶ You have my word.

我保證。

track 099

★ Thank you for being here with me.

謝謝你來陪我！

深入分析

當人失意、面臨災難的時候，最需要的是朋友或親人的陪伴，若是有人不辭辛勞地陪在你身邊安慰你、開導你、伴你度過這些痛苦的時間，請記得獻上你最誠摯的感恩之情："Thank you for being here with me."，表示「謝謝你來陪我！」

實用會話

A I feel bad about all you've been going through.

對你所經歷過的一切，我感到很抱歉。

B Thank you for being here with me, Chuck.

查克，謝謝你過來陪我！

A Hey, you're my best friend.

嘿，你是我最要好的朋友耶！

track 100

★ You're my best friend.

你是我的好朋友耶！

深入分析

當朋友面臨人生的難關時，你適時地提供肩膀依靠、陪在他邊、給他一個擁抱，都能夠幫助對方走出難關。當對方向你道感謝，你就可以說："You're my best friend."，表示朋友之間相互扶持是應該的。

實用會話

A Thank you so much for coming over.

謝謝你趕過來！

B Come on, you're my best friend.

拜託，你是我的好朋友耶！

衍生例句

▶ What are friends for?

朋友是幹什麼用的？就是要互相幫助啊！

track 101

★ I can't figure it out.

我實在想不透！

深入分析

當你想破頭還是搞不清楚一些事情的時候，就可以說："I can't figure it out."，例如明明家裡沒有其他人在，為什麼桌上的蛋糕會不翼而飛時，你就可以說："I can't figure it out."

實用會話

A Do you know why he's done this to her?

你知道他為什麼會這麼對她嗎？

B I can't figure it out.

我想不透！

實用會話

A Tell me what happened.

告訴我發生什麼事了！

B You know what? I can't figure it out.

你知道嗎？我實在想不透！

track 102

★I know.

我知道啦！

深入分析

"I know."是很簡單的一句話，表示「我知道」，但若你是用不耐煩的語氣來說，就有一點嫌對方囉囉嗦嗦了！例如兒子起床老是不摺被子、穿過的衣襪隨手亂丟等，當你要他維持好的生活習慣時，他可就會說："I know."，表示「我都知道啦！你不要再說了！」

實用會話

A Don't stay up too late doing nothing.

不要無所事事熬夜太晚喔！

B I know, mom.

媽咪，我知道啦！

A Good boy.

好孩子！（適用在小男生）

實用會話

A Did you hear me?

你有聽到我說的嗎？

B Yes, I did.

有，我有！

A Did you really understand...

你真的知道…

Ⓑ I said I know.

我說我知道啦！

徹底學會英文

Say no more.

不要再說了！

若是希望對方不要再囉唆，也可以直接說："Say no more."，表示「不要再說了！」

A：Why don't you just clean your...

你應該要整理你的…

B：Say no more. Please.

不要再說了！拜託！

A：Listen? Do you hear that? Maybe it's him.

你聽！有聽到嗎？可能是他喔！

B：Say no more. Just be quiet.

不要再說了！安靜一點！

track 103

★I knew it.

我早就知道！

深入分析

和前面的"I know."不同，當你早料到某件不好的事會發生，也警告過其他人要小心，但不幸的事仍舊發生，你就可以憤恨地說："I knew it."，意思是「我早知會有這種結果」，雖然有些馬後砲的意味，但可以表達你一絲絲的後悔之意，多半是用過去式的時態表示。

實用會話

Ⓐ I knew it. I should stop them.

我早就知道！我應該阻止他們。

Ⓑ Yes, you should.

是啊，你的確應該這麼做！

實用會話

Ⓐ Look what he's done to our daughter.

瞧他對我們的女兒做的好事！

Ⓑ See? I just knew it. We have to...

你看吧！我就知道！我們應該要…

Ⓒ Say no more, guys. Please.

二位，不要再說了！拜託！

衍生例句

► I just know it.

我就知道！

► I told you so.

我告訴過你了吧！

track 104

★ Don't try to deny it.

不要想要否認喔！

深入分析

當某人企圖否認某事，卻又被你識破時，你就可以告誡他："Don't try to deny it."，意思是「這一切我都知道了，不要想騙過我喔！」

實用會話

A Are you seeing someone now?

你現在有交往對象嗎？

B No! I'm not.

沒有！我沒有！

A Don't try to deny it.

不要想要否認喔！

實用會話

A Don't try to deny it, you think I'm stupid!

不要想要否認，你認為我是笨蛋！

B I didn't mean it.

我沒有這個意思！

track 105

★ No, I guess.

我猜沒有吧！

深入分析

當對方問你一個「是或非」的問題時，若你對答案不是很確定時，就可以回答："No, I guess."或是："Yes, I guess."，表示你自己對yes或no也不是非常有把握！

實用會話

Ⓐ Anybody know how it happened?
有人知道是怎麼發生的嗎？

Ⓑ No, I guess.
我想沒有吧！

Ⓒ They're just kids. Probably they are afraid they'll get into trouble.
他們只是孩子啊！可能怕惹上麻煩！

衍生例句

► Yes and no.
也是，也不是。

► I'm not so sure.
我不是很確定！

track 106

★ Could you just go away?

能請你離開嗎？

深入分析

中文常說的「不要理我」，英文並沒有這樣的用語，所以當你心情不好，只想一個人靜一靜、不想有人來打擾你的時候，就可以請這些讓你礙眼的人離你遠一點："Could you just go away?"

另一種發洩情緒的怒吼用語，則是："Go away."，表示「你走開！不要理我」的意思。

實用會話

A Hey, are you all right?

嘿，你還好吧？

B Could you please just go away?

能請你離開嗎？

A Come on. Is there anything I can do for you?

不要這樣嘛！有什麼需要我幫忙的嗎？

實用會話

A Just go away.

你走開！

B Come on, you need to move on.

不要這樣，你要繼續過日子啊！

徹底學會英文

Leave me alone.

讓我一個人靜一靜！

若是你只想一個人獨處，又不希望用「趕人」(Go away!)的方式請對方離開，就可以說："Leave me alone." 表示「讓我一個人獨處」，也就是「讓我一個人靜一靜！」的意思！

此外，"Leave someone alone."也有表示「放棄某人」，也就是中文「不要理某人」、「不要管某人」的意思。

A：Are you OK? You look upset.
你還好吧？你看起來有些沮喪喔！

B：What can we do for you?
我們能為你做什麼？

C：Just leave me alone.
讓我一個人靜一靜就好！

A：Mom, look what Eric did.
媽，妳看艾瑞克做的好事！

B：Just leave him alone.
不要管他！

track 107

★It's not what you think.

事情不是你所想的那樣！

深入分析

雖然中文常說「眼見為憑」，但有的時候我們不得不承認，事實不是我們所見的那樣，這時候就可以說："It's not what you think."，雖然沒有點明「不要相信你所看見的事」，但是卻有著「不管是因為親眼所見或是聽聞，事情和你所認知的不同」的辯解。

實用會話

A Listen to me, honey.

親愛的，你聽我說！

B How could you do this to me?

你怎麼能這樣對我？

A The thing with Tina it's not what you think.

和蒂娜的事，不是你所想的那樣！

衍生例句

► It's not true.

這不是事實！

► The news is true.

這個消息是真的。

track 108

★Have a drink.

去喝杯酒吧！

深入分析

若是你要邀請朋友去喝酒，可以不使用"drink"這個單字，只要說："Have a drink."就可以了！

實用會話

Ⓐ Are you busy now?

你現在忙嗎？

Ⓑ Nope. What's up?

沒有啊！有事嗎？

Ⓐ Let's have a drink.

我們去喝杯酒吧！

實用會話

Ⓐ I can't believe what he did to me.

我真是不敢相信他對我所做的事。

Ⓑ Go home. Have a drink. A big one.

回家去吧，去喝杯酒吧，要喝大杯一點！

衍生例句

► I'll buy you a drink.

我請你喝一杯。

track 109

★ For example?

例如什麼？

深入分析

中文常說：「舉個例子來聽聽」或是「例如什麼」的用法，在英文中，只要簡單地說："For example?"，這是慣用語句，就可以表達希望對方「舉個例子」或繼續說明的意思。

另外一種和中文「像什麼」很類似的說法則是："Like what?"

實用會話

Ⓐ You should buy her some flowers, or something.

你應該買個花或隨便什麼禮物給她！

Ⓑ For example?

例如什麼？

Ⓐ Something to perk her up. Candy, maybe.

可以讓她高興的東西，或許是糖果也可以。

實用會話

Ⓐ I don't know. I just wanna write something.

我不知道耶！我就是想寫一些東西。

Ⓑ Like what?

像什麼？

衍生例句

► Can you give us an example?

可以給我們一點建議嗎？

track 110

★I have a good idea!

我有一個好主意。

深入分析

當大家對某一個議題想破頭，卻仍然束手無策時，你突然靈光一現，想到一個好方法，就可以說："I have a good idea!"，或是簡單地說："I have an idea."。要記住，注意冠詞（a或an）的變換，因為"idea"是母音（aɪ　）為首的發音，所以要使用"an idea"來表示。

實用會話

Ⓐ I have a good idea!

我有一個好主意。

Ⓑ Yes?

是什麼呢？

Ⓐ Maybe I should find a part-time job.

也許我應該要找一份兼職的工作。

實用會話

Ⓐ I have an idea. Listen to this.

我有一個好主意！你聽聽！

Ⓑ Not now, OK? I'm not in that mood.

不要現在好嗎？我沒那個心情！

---

track 111

★ That's a good idea.

好主意！

深入分析

當對方提出一個想法或主意，又能得到你的認同，你就可以說："That's a good idea."，表示你贊成對方所提的主意，也可以只是簡單地說： "Good idea."

實用會話

Ⓐ Maybe you should ask her out.

也許你應該約她出去。

Ⓑ Oh, that's a good idea.

喔，好主意！

實用會話

Ⓐ What do you say?

你覺得呢？

B Wow. Good idea.
哇！好主意！

衍生例句

▶ This is great.
太好了！

track 112

★ Of course!

當然！

深入分析

「相當然爾」的中文怎麼說？不難，若是在回答的句子中使用，直接說："Of course!"就可以了！

實用會話

A Do you have any plans next weekend?
你們下個週末有事嗎？

B Yes, we're biking to Mountain Jade next weekend with some friends of mine.
有啊，下個週末我們要和一些我的朋友去玉山騎單車。

C How about joining us?
要不要和我們一起去？

A Of course, I'd love to.
當然好！我想去！

實用會話

Ⓐ Do you mean we can leave now?

你的意思是我們們現在可以走了嗎？

Ⓑ Of course!

當然！

---

track 113

★ Of course not.

當然沒有！

深入分析

當對方問你一個問題，你的回答不但是"no"，更想要強調這個否定的回答時，就可以更直接地說："Of course not."

實用會話

Ⓐ Are you gay or not?

你是同性戀嗎？

Ⓑ No, of course not. What kind of stupid question is that?

不是，當然不是啊！這是什麼笨問題？

實用會話

Ⓐ Did you go to the prom with David?

你有和大衛去舞會嗎？

Ⓑ Who? David? Of course not.

誰？大衛？當然沒有！

Ⓐ Poor guy.

可憐的傢伙！

實用會話

Ⓐ Can I go camping with Sean?

我可以和史恩去露營嗎？

Ⓑ Of course not!

當然不可以！

Ⓐ Please?

拜託啦！

Ⓑ We'll see.

再說吧！

衍生例句

▶ Absolutely not.

當然不是！

track 114

★Absolutely.

無庸置疑！

深入分析

和"Of course"一樣意思的語句，"absolutely"可以充分表達「可以」、「是的」、「沒錯」、「同意你的言論」的意思，若是否定式則直接在"absolutely"後面加"not"即可。

實用會話

Ⓐ You mean I can go to a movie with Jim tonight?

你的意思是今晚我可以和吉姆去看電影囉？

Ⓑ Absolutely.

是啊！

實用會話

Ⓐ I don't like what you are saying.

我不喜歡你說的話。

Ⓑ You don't?

你不喜歡？

Ⓐ Absolutely not.

非常不喜歡！

track 115

★I don't think so.

沒有吧！

深入分析

中文常說的「不會吧！」、「沒有吧！」，記住這個觀念：以上的否定語句都傳達了「我不這麼認為」的想法，而英文該怎麼說呢？就叫做："I don't think so."，是一句非常實用的短語。

實用會話

Ⓐ Weren't you and I in one of the same classes in college?

我們是不是在大學曾經一起上課過？

Ⓑ I don't think so.

沒有吧！

實用會話

Ⓐ Have you two met each other?

你們兩位見過面嗎？

Ⓑ I don't think so.

沒有吧！

track 116

★ You're good.

你真是棒！

深入分析

請不要吝嗇說出你的讚美，當對方表現得很優秀或是盡力表現時，你就可以誇獎："You're good."，例如兒子拾金不昧的行為，你就可以誇獎他："You're good."

實用會話

Ⓐ Take a look at this. I made this chair on my own.

你看一下這個東西！這張椅子是我自己做的！

Ⓑ Wow, you're good.

哇，你真是棒！

衍生例句

▶ It's cool.

酷喔！

▶ It's terrific.

= It's wonderful.

= It's awesome.

太好了！

track 117

★ How are you?

你好嗎？

深入分析

當你在路上偶遇熟識的人，不管是朋友、同事、親戚、鄰居等，都應該主動問候對方："How are you?"，也就是中文的「你好嗎？」的意思。

實用會話

Ⓐ Good morning! How are you?

早安！你好嗎？

Ⓑ Great. How about you?

不錯！你呢？

A I found a new job.

我找到新工作了！

B Good to hear that.

真替你感到高興！

衍生例句

▶ How do you do?

= How are you doing?

你好嗎？

track 118

★I haven't seen you in ages!

好久不見了！

深入分析

偶遇很久不見的朋友時，你的打招呼方式就應該先告訴對方："I haven't seen you in ages!"，表示「我們很久沒有見面了！」然後才是問候對方："How do you do?"，表示「你好嗎？」

實用會話

A Hi, Jim! I haven't seen you in ages!

嗨，吉姆，好久不見了！

B Carol! What a surprise!

卡蘿！真是訝異（會遇見你）！

A How are you?

你好嗎？

B Great. What have you been up to?

我很好！你最近在忙些什麼事？

衍生例句

▶ Long time no see!

好久不見！

▶ It's been a long time.

真的是好久了！

▶ How has it been going?

近來好嗎？

track 119

★ What's new?

有什麼新鮮事嗎？

深入分析

當你遇見好久不曾再見面或有好一陣子沒有消息的朋友時，就可以問問對方："What's new?"，表示「好久不見，這陣子有沒有發生什麼是我不知道的事？」是一種想要和對方分享他的近況的問候語句。

實用會話

A How do you do?

你好嗎？

B Hey, long time no see!
嘿，好久不見了！

A What's new?
有什麼新鮮事嗎？

B David and I just moved back to Seattle.
我和大衛才剛搬回西雅圖。

衍生例句

► What's up?
有什麼事嗎？

track 120

★ What have you been up to?
你最近在忙些什麼事？

深入分析

若是要關心好久不見的朋友最近在忙些什麼，就可以問："What have you been up to?"

實用會話

A Long time no see!
好久不見！

B Hello! What have you been up to?
哈囉！你最近在忙些什麼事？

A I've just been on a three-week cruise!
我才剛參加了為期三週的旅遊。

實用會話

A How nice to see you!

真高興遇見你！

B What have you been up to?

最近在忙些什麼事？

A I've been studying at Washington University.

我在華盛頓大學唸書。

衍生例句

▶ Hi! What's new?

嗨，近來好嗎？

track 121

★ It's nice seeing you.

真高興遇見你！

深入分析

遇到好久不見的朋友後，在稍微聊天之後，可以在臨道別時讓對方知道你是多麼高興能和他再見面，此時你就可以說："It's nice seeing you."

實用會話

A Well, it's getting late.

嗯，好晚了！

Ⓑ It's nice seeing you.

真高興遇見你！

Ⓐ I really must go now.

我應該要走囉！

Ⓑ OK. See you soon.

好吧！再見囉！

Ⓐ Bye.

再見！

衍生例句

► It's been a pleasure talking with you.

真高興和你聊天！

track 122

★ It's been nice talking to you.

很高興和你聊天！

深入分析

當你和外國友人聊天聊了一段時間後，對方說："It's been nice talking to you."，除了是表達他很高興能和你聊天的這一段時間之外，也暗示你他準備要說再見了，所以接下來他就會說有其他事、要趕時間、時間很晚了…等的理由，要說再見囉！

實用會話

Ⓐ It's late now.

現在很晚了！

Ⓑ Sure. It's been nice talking to you.
沒錯！很高興和你聊天！

Ⓐ OK. I've got to leave now.
好吧！我現在得要走了！

Ⓑ Bye.
再見！

實用會話

Ⓐ It's been nice talking to you, Karen.
凱倫，很高興和妳聊天！

Ⓑ I've enjoyed talking to you, too, Jim.
我也很高興和你聊天，吉姆！

Ⓐ Good luck on your interview.
希望妳面試有好運！

Ⓑ Thanks. I really want this job.
謝謝！我真的想要這份工作！

衍生例句

► Nice talking to you.
很高興和你聊天！

track 123

★I'm afraid I have to be going.

恐怕我該走了！

深入分析

當你準備要和閒聊的對方說再見時，可以先暗示他：「我該走了」，英文就叫做："I'm afraid I have to be going."，你也可以直接說："I have to be going."，表示你準備要說再見了！

實用會話

Ⓐ Well, I'm afraid I have to be going.

是這樣的，我恐怕該走了！

Ⓑ I know you are busy, so I'll let you go.

我知道你很忙，先說再見囉！

Ⓐ See you lalter.

再見囉！

Ⓑ See you.

再見！

實用會話

Ⓐ I have to be going.

我要走囉！

Ⓑ OK. See you tomorrow.

好吧！明天見！

track 124

★We have some catching up to do.

我們可以好好聊一聊！

深入分析

遇見好久不見的老朋友時，你希望兩人能一起坐下來好好聊聊，就可以說："We have some catching up to do."，其中"some catching up to do"是慣用語。

實用會話

A Have you got time for coffee?
有空喝杯咖啡嗎？

B Sure! That sounds great.
好啊！不錯的建議耶！

A We have some catching up to do.
我們可以好好聊一聊！

track 125

★Why don't we get some coffee somewhere?

我們何不找個地方喝杯咖啡？

深入分析

當你巧遇許久不見的朋友，一定會說「我們聊一聊吧！」以邀約對方一起聚會，美國人則習慣用「喝杯咖啡」邀約："get some coffee somewhere"，表示「找個地方喝杯咖啡」的意思，可能不用特別約，「現在就到街角的咖啡廳喝杯咖啡」的意思。

實用會話

Ⓐ Listen, why don't we get some coffee somewhere?

聽好，我們何不找個地方喝杯咖啡？

Ⓑ Oh, I'd love to, but I've got to get going.

喔，我很想啊！可是我要走了！

Ⓐ How about dinner? You and your wife can meet me after my class.

要不要一起吃個晚餐？你和你太太在我下課後來找我！

Ⓑ Sounds great.

聽起來不錯喔！

實用會話

Ⓐ Why don't we get some coffee somewhere?

我們何不找個地方喝杯咖啡？

Ⓑ Good idea. Let's go to the coffee shop on the corner.

好主意！我們去轉角的咖啡店吧！

track 126

★What a surprise.

好巧啊！

深入分析

雖然"What a surprise."的字面意思是「真是訝異」，但通常可以和中文所描述「好巧啊！」的情境相通，表示現在所面臨的狀況是非預期會發生，是非常令人訝異的意思。

實用會話

Ⓐ Jim Smith? Oh my, what a surprise.
吉姆・史密斯？喔，我的天啊！好巧啊！

Ⓑ I don't believe it. What are you doing here in Seattle?
我真是不敢相信！你怎麼會在西雅圖？

Ⓐ I just spent a few days with my parents.
我這幾天來探望我的父母！

實用會話

Ⓐ Hey, look, here comes David.
嘿，你看！大衛來了！

Ⓑ Hi, David.
嗨，大衛。

Ⓒ What a surprise. What are you guys doing here?
好巧啊！你們大家在這裡做什麼？

Ⓑ We're going to see a movie.

我們要去看電影。

Ⓐ Yeah. Do you wanna come?

是啊！你要去嗎？

track 127

★I'm on my way.

我正在去的路上。

深入分析

當你約會快要遲到時，得趕緊打電話告訴對方："I'm on my way."，說明「我正在路上了」，這是為了傳遞你「快到了」或是「已經出發」的訊息。

實用會話

Ⓐ Carol, would you do me a favor?

卡蘿，可以幫我一個忙嗎？

Ⓑ Sure. What is it?

好啊！什麼事？

Ⓐ Would you call Mr. Dow? I'm supposed to meet him at three.

你可以打電話給道爾先生嗎？我應該要在三點鐘和他碰面。

Ⓑ No problem.

沒問題！

Ⓐ Tell him I'm on my way.

告訴他我正在去的路上。

track 128

★I'm on my way home.

我正在回家的路上。

深入分析

上一句"on my way"是說明「在去程的路上」，卻沒有說明目的地在哪裡。若是指「在回家的路上」，則可以說"on my way home"，但若是指"home"以外的其他地方，則應該在way的後面加上"to＋目的地"的說明，例如："I'm on my way to the museum."（我正在去博物館的路上）

實用會話

Ⓐ Where are you off to?

你要去哪裡？

Ⓑ I'm on my way home.

我正在回家的路上。你呢？

實用會話

Ⓐ Jim? Where are you going?

吉姆？你要去哪裡？

Ⓑ I'm on my way to the shopping mall.

我正在要去賣場的路上。

Ⓐ OK. See you later.

瞭解！再見囉！

衍生例句

► I'm on my way to the grocery store.

我正在去雜貨店的路上。

track 129

★I'm on my way back to New York.

我正在要回紐約的路上。

深入分析

當你在去某個地點的路上時，可以說"on my way to＋地點"，而若是特指「在『回去』某地的路上」時，則可以在way的後面加上back（回程），表示「回去某地的路上」。

實用會話

Ⓐ Gee, it's been a long time.

天啊！真的是好久了！

Ⓑ Sure, it has.

是啊！的確是！

Ⓐ Where are you going?

你要去哪裡？

B I'm on my way back to New York.

我正在要回紐約的路上。

實用會話

A Hi, Jim, where are you going?

嗨，吉姆，你要去哪裡？

B I'm on my way back to the United States.

我要回去美國。

track 130

★It's freezing today.

今天真的冷斃了！

深入分析

我們在路上遇到熟識的人時，如果接近用餐時間，一定會問「吃飽了嗎？」來打開話匣子，但是美國人很少會這麼問，他們常說的是和天氣相關的聊天話題，例如："What a fine day."，表示「天氣真好」。

實用會話

A It's freezing today, isn't it?

今天真的冷斃了，對吧？

B You're not kidding!

你說得沒錯！

實用會話

A Boy, it's so cold.

老天！真冷！

B Yeah, it's chilly, but I like it.

是啊！冷斃了！可是我愛極了！

衍生例句

► What lovely weather!

今天天氣真好！

► What horrible weather!

這是什麼鬼天氣！

track 131

★ That's news to me.

這可是新聞呢！

深入分析

若是某則消息對你來說是從未聽聞過的，中文就會說：「這對我來說是新鮮事」，英文就叫做："That's news to me."，此外，也可以表示「我不知道有這件事」或「我沒有被告知」。

實用會話

A You know what? Jim got a promotion.

你知道嗎？吉姆升官了！

Ⓑ Really? That's news to me.

真的嗎？這可是新聞呢！

實用會話

Ⓐ Jim told me he did a lot of cooking.

吉姆有告訴我他煮了很多飯。

Ⓑ Well, that's news to me.

是喔，這可是新聞呢！

實用會話

Ⓐ The telephones are out. None of them work.

電話壞了！全都壞了！

Ⓑ That's news to me.

我倒是不知道有這件事！

---

track 132

★ You what?

你說什麼？

深入分析

當對方說了一件不可思議的事，你就可以佯裝好似聽不懂他所說的話，中文就會說：「你說什麼？」，而英文就叫做："You what?"，表示對方的言論讓你不敢恭維或不敢相信！

此外，"You what?"也帶有一絲希望對方再說一次的意思。

實用會話

A Should I broke up with Jim?

我應該和吉姆分手嗎？

B You what?

你說什麼？

A I know he is not my soul mate.

我知道他不是我的心靈伴侶！

實用會話

A I should have...

我應該要…

B You what?

你說什麼？

A Never mind.

算了！

track 133

★ It's your own fault.

這是你自己造成的錯誤！

深入分析

若是對方咎由自取，你就有十足的理由責問對方，並告訴他這是他自己造成的："It's your own fault."，表示「錯不在別人，而是你自己！」

實用會話

Ⓐ You look pale.
你看起來臉色蒼白！

Ⓑ Damn, I'm so tired.
真是的！我好累！

Ⓐ It's your own fault. You shouldn't stay up all night.
這是你自己造成的錯誤！你不應該整晚熬夜！

衍生例句

▶ You have no one but yourself to blame.
你自己的錯自己承擔！

▶ You have only yourself to blame.
你怪不得別人！

track 134

★ Don't blame yourself.

不要自責！

深入分析

當某件不好的事情發生時，你自覺是自己應該要負責而自責不已時，周遭的人就可以安慰你："Don't blame yourself."

實用會話

Ⓐ What happened here?

這裡發生了什麼事？

Ⓑ I'm really sorry about that.

對那件事我真的很抱歉！

Ⓐ Don't blame yourself. It's not your fault.

不要自責！不是你的錯！

衍生例句

► It's not your fault.

不是你的錯！

track 135

★ No, why?

不會啊！為什麼這麼問？

深入分析

先否定對方的問題後，再追問原因的情境下，就可以說："No, why?"，不僅僅是回答對方的問題，你更要知道對方為什麼會這麼問。

相反的用法則為"Yes, why?"，表示「是啊！為什麼這麼問？」

實用會話

Ⓐ Are you busy now?

你現在忙嗎？

B No, why?

不會啊！有事嗎？

A Do you wanna go to a movie with me?

你要和我去看電影嗎？

實用會話

A Did you call Sandy last night?

你昨天有打電話給珊蒂嗎？

B Yes, why?

有啊！為什麼這麼問？

A She and I, we were... You know.

她和我，我們…。你知道的啦！

---

track 136

★They're nothing special.

沒什麼特別啦！

深入分析

有人稱讚你時，你是不是會謙虛地說「沒什麼啦！」、「哪裡！」，同樣的情境中，英文就可以說："They're nothing special."，表示「都是普通的小事」，實在沒有什麼值得宣揚的意思！

實用會話

A You know, Karen, you make the best pork chops in the whole world.

凱倫，妳知道嗎？妳做的豬排是全世界最好吃的。

B Oh, Jim, they're nothing special.

喔！吉姆，這沒什麼特別啦！

track 137

★This is nothing.

這沒什麼啦！

深入分析

和上一句的情境很類似，除了是表示「謙虛」的一種回答，也可以表示所遭遇的事情不足掛齒的意思。

實用會話

A Isn't it too hard for you?

對你來說會不會很難？

B Come on, this is nothing.

拜託，這沒什麼！

A Oh, good.

喔，好吧！

實用會話

A Wow, did you make this on your own?

哇！這是你自己做的嗎？

B Yeah. How do you like it?

是啊！你喜歡嗎？

A Very much. Thank you so much.

非常喜歡！真是太謝謝你了！

B Oh, this is nothing.

喔，這沒什麼啦！

---

track 138

★ I can't put it down.

我欲罷不能！

深入分析

當你讀到一本好書，實在是「欲罷不能」時，該怎麼表達？很簡單，這就是「這本書實在是吸引我到無法放下這本書」的情境，就是「欲罷不能」，這樣一來就不難理解"I can't put it down."的用法囉！

實用會話

A I see you're reading "Over the Top."How do you like it?

我看你在看Over the Top這本書。你喜歡嗎？

B I can't put it down.

我欲罷不能！

A Have you read it?

你有看過嗎？

B I just finished it. The ending is great.

我才剛看完！結局很棒！

track 139

★Very much.

的確是非常！

深入分析

當你要強調某事的狀況時，可以在對方提問之後，回答"Very much."，表示「非常」意思，通常是在對方問你「是否喜歡…」，你就可以回答 "Very much."，是屬於非常簡單的口語化語句。

"Very much."也適用在和完整句子連用，當成副詞形容整個句子，例如："I like it very much."（我非常喜歡）

實用會話

Ⓐ Are you from New York?

你來自紐約嗎？

Ⓑ Well, I'm originally from Seattle, but I live in New York now.

嗯，我原來是來自西雅圖，但我現在住紐約。

Ⓐ How do you like New York?

你喜歡紐約嗎？

Ⓑ Very much.

非常喜歡！

實用會話

Ⓐ Thank you very much.

非常謝謝你！

Ⓑ You're welcome.

不客氣！

實用會話

Ⓐ How was the camping?

露營好玩嗎？

Ⓑ We enjoyed ourselves very much.

我們玩得非常高興！

track 140

★ By the way, I'm Jim.

對了，我叫吉姆。

深入分析

當聊天到某個時機點時，如果你想要轉換話題，中文常說：「對了，…」，以提醒對方你打算轉換話題或提醒對方注意你接下來要說的事，具有銜接不同話題的作用，英文就叫做："By the way, ..."。

實用會話

Ⓐ Don't you think this is great?

你不覺得這個很棒嗎？

Ⓑ Yes, it is.

是啊，的確是！

Ⓐ By the way, I'm Jim.

對了，我叫吉姆。

Ⓑ Nice talking to you, Jim.

很高興和你聊天，吉姆。

實用會話

Ⓐ Great party, isn't it? By the way, I'm Jim.

這個派對很好玩，對吧？對了，我叫吉姆。

Ⓑ Hi, I'm Carol, and this is my husband David.

嗨，我是卡蘿，這位是我丈夫大衛。

實用會話

Ⓐ I'm so exhausted.

我累斃了！

Ⓑ Let's call it a day.

今天就到這裡為止吧！

Ⓐ Oh, by the way, did you send David our sales report?

喔！對了，你有寄給大衛我們的銷售報表嗎？

Ⓑ Yes, I sent it to him last week.

有的，我上週就寄給他了！

track 141

★ Have you ever been to New York?

你有來過紐約嗎？

深入分析

若是以前曾經發生過的事，通常是用「過去式」的語法，但若是強調「是否曾經歷過的經驗」，則多半是使用「完成式」的語法，最常見的句型是："have you ever..."，表示詢問「你是否曾經…」的經歷。

實用會話

Ⓐ Have you ever been to New York?
你有到過紐約嗎？

Ⓑ No, I haven't. This is my first trip.
沒有，我沒來過！這是我第一次來！

實用會話

Ⓐ Have you ever been to Taiwan?
你有到過台灣嗎？

Ⓑ Yes. As a matter of fact, my husband is Taiwanese.
有啊！事實上，我先生是台灣人！

Ⓐ Really? How do you like its food?
真的嗎？妳喜歡台灣的飲食嗎？

🅑 Well, it depends on.
嗯，看情況耶！

track 142

★ The entire thing was a joke.

這整件事真是個笑話！

深入分析

好幾年前的某一樁政治事件，港星成龍的一句「這真是個天大的笑話」言論，就可以用"The entire thing was a joke."詮釋，表示「這件事從頭到尾都是不可思議」的意思。

實用會話

🅐 This is how we make it up.
我們就是這樣彌補的。

🅑 I didn't insult you. The entire thing was a joke.
我無意冒犯。這整件事真是個笑話！

🅐 I'm so sorry to hear that.
真是遺憾！

衍生例句

► It's ridiculous.
真是荒謬！

track 143

★I didn't insult you.

我無意冒犯你！

深入分析

當人在激烈辯論時，常常會口不擇言，或是「言者無心聽者有意」，因此造成更大的衝突或誤會，此時你可以先聲明：「我無意冒犯」，英文就叫做："I didn't insult you."

實用會話

Ⓐ I'm not playing your games.

我不玩了！

Ⓑ You what?

什麼嘛！

Ⓐ Hey, I didn't insult you.

嘿，我無意冒犯你！

Ⓑ But you just did.

可是你剛剛就是冒犯我了！

實用會話

Ⓐ I didn't call you a moron or anything.

我沒有說你是白癡或其他稱號！

Ⓑ Yes, you do.

有，你有！

Ⓐ Sorry, I didn't insult you.

抱歉，我無意冒犯你！

---

track 144

★It isn't getting any better.

事情並沒有好轉，對嗎。

深入分析

若是表示「事情漸入佳境」，英文就叫做"get better"，表示「情況好轉」，better是good或fine的比較級用語。

反之，「情況每況愈下」時，就可以說"get worse"。

實用會話

Ⓐ It just isn't getting any better, is it?
事情並沒有好轉，對嗎？

Ⓑ I'm afraid not.
恐怕是如此！

實用會話

Ⓐ How's it going?
事情順利嗎？

Ⓑ It's not getting any better.
事情並沒有好轉。

Ⓐ Why? What happened? What did you do?
為什麼？發生什麼事了？你們做了什麼事？

Ⓑ We did nothing.
我們什麼也沒做！

實用會話

A How bad is it?

情況有多糟？

B It's getting worse.

越來越不樂觀了！

衍生例句

▶ Things are getting better.

情況有正在好轉。

track 145

★I guess so.

我想是吧！

深入分析

當你不確定某件事時，中文會說：「應該是吧！」或「我想是吧！」英文就叫做："I guess so."，字面意思是「我猜測的確是如此」，會在字尾出現"so"，表示之前已有人發表過相關的言論了，你只是順著那個講法附和罷了，但帶有些許不確定的態度！

實用會話

A Are you ready to leave?

你要準備走了嗎？

B I guess so.

我想是吧！

實用會話

Ⓐ Don't you think this is putting the cart before the horse?

你不覺得這是本末倒置嗎？

Ⓑ I guess so.

我想是吧！

實用會話

Ⓐ Doesn't that sound great?

聽起來不是很有趣嗎？

Ⓑ I guess so.

好像是吧！

衍生例句

▶ I think so.

我是這麼認為的！

▶ Perhaps.

或許吧！

▶ Maybe.

有可能！

track 146

★I'm afraid so.

恐怕是如此！

深入分析

當對方發表某個論點或結論，而你也認同時，就可以說："I'm afraid so."，表示「應該是如此」，但也帶有一點「我不是百分之百確認」的意味。

實用會話

A Well, you know what they say, "No news is good news."

是這樣的，人們常說：「沒有消息就是好消息！」

B I'm afraid so.

恐怕是如此！

實用會話

A You didn't get the job, did you?

你沒有得到那份工作，對嗎？

B I'm afraid so.

恐怕是如此！

A Oh, sorry to hear that.

喔，好遺憾喔！

track 147

★Sounds great.

聽起來不錯耶！

深入分析

相較於"I guess so."這種不確定性的附和用語，"Sounds great."則是對於對方所提的建議表示支持與讚賞，例如當朋友建議週末大家一起找個氣氛不錯的餐廳聚餐時，你就可以說："Sounds great."，完整的說法是"It sounds great."

此外，上述的常用句型是"It sounds..."，表示「聽起來…」，後面可以加形容詞或名詞，以附和所聽到的句子。

實用會話

Ⓐ How about having dinner with us, both of you?

要不要和我們一起去吃晚餐？你們一起來！

Ⓑ Sounds great.

聽起來不錯耶！

Ⓒ Well, I was planning to work...

嗯，我打算要工作耶…

實用會話

Ⓐ Maybe we can go shopping tonight.

也許我們今晚可以去逛街！

Ⓑ Sounds good.

聽起來不錯耶！

A OK. I'll pick you up at five.

好！我五點鐘去接你！

B Sure. See you then.

好！到時候見囉！

實用會話

A It'll go faster this way.

這樣會比較快！

B It sounds great.

聽起來不錯喔！

實用會話

A Maybe you can come with us.

也許你可以和我們一起去！

B That sounds like a good idea.

聽起是個好主意喔！

衍生例句

▶ Good idea.

好主意！

徹底學會英文

Not such a good idea for me.

聽起來對我來說不是個好主意！

當你不認同對方的觀點或想法時，若是不想直接說："This is not a good idea."，你就可以直接站在自己的立場說明："Not such a good idea for me."，是指「聽起來對我來說不是個好主意」，表示「對我來說不好，但是我不知你的想法（或大家的想法）如何？」

A：Why don't we just watch TV and do nothing.
我們何不就看電視，然後什麼事都不要做！

B：Not such a good idea for me.
聽起來對我來說不是個好主意！

track 148

★Where are you off to?

你要去哪裡？

深入分析

當你在路上偶遇行色匆匆的朋友時，就可以問問他："Where are you off to?"，表示「你要去哪裡？」是一句非常道地的閒聊招呼用語。

實用會話

A Jim?
吉姆？

B Hi, Karen, where are you off to?
嗨，凱倫！妳要去哪裡？

A I'm going to the park.
我要去公園！

實用會話

Ⓐ Where are you guys off to?

你們大家要去哪裡？

Ⓑ We're taking a trip to Seattle.

我們要去一趟西雅圖！

衍生例句

▶ Where are you going?

你要去哪裡？

track 149

★ Have fun.

好好玩！

深入分析

當得知同事準備要放長假時，中文會說：「好好去玩吧！」英文就可以說："Have fun."，或是兒子準備要去參加三天兩夜的露營時，你也可以說：" Have fun."

實用會話

Ⓐ I'm taking a few days off. I'm going to visit some of my friends.

我要休幾天假！我要去拜訪我的一些朋友！

Ⓑ Have fun.

好好玩！

實用會話

Ⓐ Do you have any plans this weekend?
你這個週末有什麼計畫嗎？

Ⓑ Yes. We're going on a picnic.
有！我們要去野餐！

Ⓐ OK. Have fun.
好吧！要玩得開心喔！

衍生例句

► Enjoy yourself!
祝你玩得開心！

track 150

★ I really enjoyed myself.

我玩得很開心。

深入分析

要表示自己真的玩得很開心，就可以說："I really enjoyed myself."，凡是表示「度過一段很快樂的時光」時，都可以說："I enjoyed myself."，因為是過去已經發生的事，所以通常是使用過去式句型。

實用會話

Ⓐ How's the party?
派對好玩嗎？

Ⓑ I really enjoyed myself.
我玩得很開心。

實用會話

Ⓐ I really enjoyed myself last night.

昨天晚上我玩得很開心！

Ⓑ Really? I'm so glad to hear that.

真的嗎？我很高興聽你這麼說！

衍生例句

► I had a good time.

我玩得很開心！

track 151

★ Are you gaining weight?

你是不是變胖了？

深入分析

"gain weight"是常用片語，表示「變胖」、「體重增加」，例如遇到久未見面的友人時，若是對方的體重明顯增加不少，你就可以試著詢問："Are you gaining weight?"。但是因為女性對自己的體重普遍都很在意，最好還是不要隨便問不熟的朋友喔！

實用會話

Ⓐ Are you gaining weight?

你是不是變胖了？

Ⓑ So obviously?

有這麼明顯嗎？

A I guess a little exercise would do you good.

稍微運動一下對你來說應該不錯！

實用會話

A Jim?

吉姆嗎？

B Hi, Karen. How are you doing?

嗨，凱倫！妳好嗎？

A Good. You look so...

很好！你看起來好…

B I know. I'm gaining weight.

我知道！我變胖了！

衍生例句

► Are you losing weight?

你變瘦了嗎？

► You've lost some weight since the last time I saw you.

從上次見到你到現在，你瘦了好多！

track 152

★You're in great shape.

你的身材看起很棒耶！

深入分析

當遇到久未見面的朋友，對方身形看起來結實、纖瘦等，都可以說："You're in great shape."，只要是和你印象中體型、外表明顯變得較好的狀況下都適用！

實用會話

Ⓐ Hi, Jim.
嗨，吉姆。

Ⓑ Karen! Hey, you've lost a lot of weight.
凱倫！嘿，妳瘦好多喔！

Ⓐ Thirty pounds.
30磅。

Ⓑ No kidding. You're in great shape.
真的假的？妳的身材看起很棒耶！

實用會話

Ⓐ Hello, Jim. You look good.
哈囉，吉姆。你看起來氣色不錯耶！

Ⓑ Thank you.
謝謝！

Ⓐ You're in great shape too.
你的身材看起來也很棒耶！

🅑 Well, I do a lot of exercise.

是這樣的，我做了很多運動！

衍生例句

▶ You look great.

你看起來氣色很好！

▶ You look beautiful.

你看起來很漂亮！

track 153

★ I'll treat.

我請客！

深入分析

想要請對方吃飯怎麼說？你可以說："I'll treat."，字面意思是「我會招待」，也就是「我來請客！」的意思。

若是在結帳的時候表明請客的意願，則可以說："It's on me."，表示「帳單就算我的吧！」

實用會話

🅐 I'm so hungry.

我好餓喔！

🅑 Maybe we can order out for pizza. I'll treat.

也許我們可以吃外送披薩。我請客！

🅐 Sounds great.

聽起來不錯喔！

實用會話

A Check, please.

請買單！

B It's on me.

帳單就算我的吧！

A Are you sure?

你確定嗎？

衍生例句

▶ My treat.

我請客。

▶ I'll treat you.

我請客。

▶ Let me treat you.

我請你。

track 154

★ How about you?

你呢？

深入分析

詢問對方的意見時，除了"What do you think of it?"之外，若你先前已經問過第一人了，此時可以不必再重複問句，而直接問："How about you?"，表示「你的答案是什麼？」的意思，翻譯文中的「答案」，可以依照實際的情況作不同的解讀，例如想法、決定…等。

實用會話

Ⓐ How do you do?

你好嗎？

Ⓑ I'm fine, thank you. How about you?

我很好，謝謝你。你呢？

Ⓐ So-so.

馬馬虎虎。

實用會話

Ⓐ I'd like to order New York Steak. Well done.

我要點紐約牛排。全熟！

Ⓑ A New York Steak, well done. How about you, sir?

一客紐約牛排，要全熟。先生，您呢？

Ⓒ I want the same.

我要點一樣的！

衍生例句

► And you?

你呢？

track 155

★What about you?

你呢？

深入分析

詢問對方的決定除了"how about you"之外，也可以用"What about you?"來表示。

實用會話

A What about you?

你呢？

B Well, I have no idea.

嗯，我不知道耶！

A Me neither.

我也是。

實用會話

A I'll have the onion soup.

我要點洋蔥湯。

B What about you, sir?

先生，您呢？

C I might have that too.

我也要點和那個一樣的。

---

track 156

★What about having a pizza first?

你看要不要先吃點比薩？

深入分析

當你要詢問對方的想法時，中文常說：「你看要不要…」英文就可以說："what about..."，通常要在about後面加名詞或動名詞，例如："what about another beer?"，表示「要不要再喝一杯啤酒？」

此外，"what about..."也可以表示詢問某人或某事物的狀況，例如："what about David?"，表示「大衛怎麼了？」

實用會話

A I don't know what to order.

我不知道要點什麼耶！

B What about having a pizza first?

你看要不要先吃點比薩？

A Oh, I don't think so.

喔，我不要！

實用會話

A What's your idea?

你的想法呢？

B What about going to the beach?

要不要先去海邊？

實用會話

Ⓐ What about that?

那個怎麼樣？

Ⓑ Well, I have no idea.

這個嘛…我沒有想法耶！

track 157

★ Never mind.

不要緊！

深入分析

若是對方不小心踩到你而向你道歉，你可以回答：「沒關係！」（It's all right），也可以說「不要緊」，比較符合這類的英文就是"Never mind."，表示「不必在意」的意思。

此外，若是你話說了一半，不想繼續說，而對方又一直問你剛剛說了什麼（What did you just say?），你也可以說："Never mind."，表示「算了！」代表你不想再提及的意思。

實用會話

Ⓐ Sorry about that.

抱歉！

Ⓑ Never mind.

不要緊。

實用會話

A What do you mean by that?

你那是什麼意思？

B Never mind what I said, it wasn't important.

不用在意我說的，一點都不重要！

徹底學會英文

Forget it.

休想！

"Forget it!"可以和"Never mind!"做相同的解釋：「算了！」，也可以表示告誡對方「想都別想」或「休想」的阻止意味！此外，按照"Forget it."的字面意思，也有「忘記它」的意思，也就是引伸為「放棄、不管」或「沒關係」的意思。

A：I really wanna...
我真的想要…

B：Listen, forget it, OK?
聽著，休想，知道嗎？

A：I'm sorry I was late.
抱歉我遲到了！

B：Forget it.
沒關係！

track 158

★No one knows.

沒有人知道。

深入分析

「我不知道」的英文是"I don't know."，但若要表達「所有的人都不知道」，則英文就可以說："No one knows."，表示「沒有人知道」。值得一提的是，"no one"表示第三人稱單數，要用單數動詞表示。

實用會話

A Do you know how it happened?

你知道如何發生的嗎？

B No, I wasn't there.

不知道，我人不在那裡！

A How about the neighbors?

鄰居呢？

B No one knows.

沒有人知道。

A Shit.

糟糕！

衍生例句

▶ Nobody knows that.

不會有人知道！

track 159

★ The whole world knows that.

全世界都知道。

深入分析

當秘密已經不是秘密，而是公開的新聞時，就表示「全世界都知道」，英文就可以說："The whole world knows that."，表示「人人都知道」的意思。

實用會話

A Did you tell dad?

你有告訴老爸嗎？

B Yeap.

有啊！

A Mom?

媽咪呢？

B Sure.

當然！

A Damn it.

可惡耶！

B The whole world knows that.

全世界都知道啦！

A Shit.

糟糕！

track 160

★ Not yet.

還沒！

深入分析

若對方問你：「是否已經…」，而你的回答是「還沒」、「尚未」時，就可以說："Not yet."，表示「還沒有發生」的意思。"Not yet."通常在回答問句的句子中使用。

實用會話

A Have you called Mr. Smith?

你有打電話給史密斯先生嗎？

B Not yet.

還沒！

實用會話

A Did you figure it out?

你有想出來嗎？

B Not yet.

還沒！

實用會話

A Is dinner ready?

晚餐準備好了嗎？

B Not yet.

還沒有！

track 161

★ Good morning.

早安。

深入分析

當你一早遇到朋友、剛上班遇到同事或主管，都應該打聲招呼，此時就非常適合說："Good morning."表示「早安」的意思！

實用會話

Ⓐ Good morning, Jim.
吉姆，早安。

Ⓑ Good morning, Mr. Smith.
早安，史密斯先生。

Ⓐ What's the rush?
你在趕什麼？

Ⓑ I'm gonna catch the plane.
我要去趕搭飛機！

衍生例句

► Good afternoon.
午安。

► Have a good day.
祝你今天好運！

track 162

★ Good evening.

晚安！

深入分析

在晚上的時間，見面的打招呼方式就改為說「晚安」，英文就可以說："Good evening."，要注意的一點是，若是屬於道別或臨睡前的道別，中文都是說「晚安」，英文就必須說："Good night."

實用會話

A Good evening.

晚安！

B Good evening, Mrs. Smith.

史密斯太太，晚安！

A Oh, it's so good to see you here. You haven't changed a bit.

喔！真高興在這裡看到你！你一點都沒變啊！

實用會話

A Good evening, Mr. Smith. Sorry I'm late.

史密斯先生，晚安！抱歉我遲到了！

B It's OK. Come on in.

沒關係！進來吧！

---

track 163

★ Good night.

晚安。

深入分析

中文的「晚安」說法只有一種，但英文則有兩種說法，一種是晚上見面的打招呼："Good evening."，而睡覺前或晚上的道別時，則是使用："Good night."

實用會話

Ⓐ I'm so tired.
我好累喔！

Ⓑ It's late now. You should go to bed.
現在很晚了！你應該上床睡覺了！

Ⓐ OK.
好吧！

Ⓑ Good night. Don't let the bedbugs bite.
晚安。祝你睡得安穩！

實用會話

Ⓐ I wanna go to bed. Good night.
我想要去睡覺了！晚安。

Ⓑ Good night.
晚安。

track 164

★ How was your day?

你今天過得如何？

深入分析

丈夫剛下班回來，你就可以關心地問：「你今天過得如何？」，純粹是表達想要多瞭解對方「今天過得是否順利」的語句，通常是用過去式表示。

實用會話

Ⓐ How was your day?
你今天過得如何？

Ⓑ I got a raise!
我加薪了！

實用會話

Ⓐ How was your day?
你今天過得如何？

Ⓑ You'll never believe what happened to me today.
你一定不相信我今天發生什麼事了！

Ⓐ Try me.
說來聽聽！

衍生例句

▶ How was your week?
你這個星期過得如何？

track 165

★How was your summer?

你的暑假過得好嗎？

深入分析

若是在假期之後與朋友碰面，就非常適合用相關的假期話題和對方打招呼，例如："How was your summer?"，表示「你的這個暑假過得如何」，要記住，因為是問過去發生的事，所以動詞要用過去式的時態。

實用會話

A Hi, Jim! How was your summer?
嗨，吉姆！你的暑假過得好嗎？

B Great.
棒透了！

實用會話

A How was your vacation?
你的假期過得好嗎？

B Terrible.
糟透了！

A What happened?
發生什麼事啦？

衍生例句

▶ How was your trip?
你的旅遊過得如何？

track 166

★How's it going?

事情順利嗎？

深入分析

當你知道對方正在進行一件事，例如一份報告、和女朋友的關係、就可以關心這件事的進度。

實用會話

Ⓐ How's it going?

事情順利嗎？

Ⓑ So-so.

馬馬虎虎。

實用會話

Ⓐ How's it going, man?

伙伴，事情順利嗎？

Ⓑ It's going pretty well.

很順利。

衍生例句

▶ How's everything?

一切還好吧？

track 167

★ Why don't you take a break?

你何不休息一下？

深入分析

"take a break"的字面意思是「拿一個中斷」，引伸為「稍微喘口氣，休息一下」的意思，例如對方說："I'm exhausted."（我累斃了！），你就可以勸勸對方：「你應該稍微休息一下」，英文就可以說："You should take a break."

實用會話

A I'm so tired. I can't think straight.
我累得無法清醒地思考問題了。

B Why don't you take a break?
你何不休息一下？

A I just can't.
我沒辦法啊！

實用會話

A Let's call it a day.
今天就到此為止！

B I really need to take a break.
我真的要休息一下了！

B Come on, let's drink some coffee. I'll treat.
走吧！我們去喝點咖啡！我請客！

track 168

★I'm worn out!

我累壞了！

深入分析

若要表達「我很累」，可以說："I'm tired."，而若是呼應「累斃了」這種口語說法，則可以說："I'm worn out!"，worn是wear的過去分詞，表示和衣服一樣穿到變舊了，形容在人的身上就是「精疲力竭」的意思。

實用會話

A You look terrible.

你看起來糟透了！

B I'm worn out!

我累壞了！

A You should take a break.

你應該要休息一下！

實用會話

A I'm home, honey. I'm worn out!

我回來了！親愛的，我累壞了！

B Why don't you take a shower?

你何不先沖個澡？

衍生例句

▶ I'm exhausted.

我累斃了！

track 169

★I'm great.

我很好。

深入分析

當對方問候你時，通常制式的回答是「我很好」，英文就可以說："I'm great."，也可以簡短地說："Fine"，要注意的是，對方若只是寒暄式地打招呼，也許他不是真的想要知道你的近況，若你也沒有特別要向對方解釋自己的近況時，也可以說：" Great, thanks. How about you?"，表示「我不錯，謝謝關心！你好嗎？」

實用會話

Ⓐ How are you today?
今天好嗎？

Ⓑ I'm great.
我很好。

實用會話

Ⓐ How do you do?
你好嗎？

Ⓑ I'm great, thank you. How about you?
我很好，謝謝你。你呢？

Ⓐ I'm fine, too.
我也很好。

track 170

★ Not bad.

還不錯！

深入分析

當有人向你寒暄問候，而你的狀況很好時，就可以說："Not bad."，表示「不差」，也就是「很好」、「滿意」的意思，也可以用"not too bad"表示。

此外，若是對方提一個問題請教你的意見，若你覺得「不錯」，也可以用"Not bad."表示。

實用會話

Ⓐ How are you doing?

你好嗎？

Ⓑ Not bad.

還不錯！

實用會話

Ⓐ What do you think of it?

你覺得呢？

Ⓑ Hmmm..., not too bad.

嗯…還不錯！

衍生例句

▶ Pretty good.

很好！

track 171

★ So far, so good.

目前還不錯。

深入分析

回答對方的問候語有許多種，若是表示「目前為止還不錯！」的意思，就可以說："So far, so good."

實用會話

A How are you today?
你今天好嗎？

B So far, so good.
目前還不錯。

實用會話

A How was your week?
你這個星期過得如何？

B So far, so good.
目前還不錯。

衍生例句

► So-so.
馬馬虎虎過得去！

track 172

★ Take care!

保重！

深入分析

當你和朋友短暫交談臨要道別時，通常會說：「多多保重！」英文就可以說："Take care!"。特別注意的是，"Take care!"這個祝福用語，通常適用在彼此可能會有一段時間不會再見面的場合中使用。

實用會話

Ⓐ There comes my bus. Bye.

我等的公車來了！再見！

Ⓑ Good-bye. Take care!

再見！保重！

實用會話

Ⓐ Take care! OK?

要保重！好嗎？

Ⓑ I will.

我會的！

Ⓐ I'm gonna miss you, sweetie.

親愛的，我會很想念你的！

衍生例句

► Take care of yourself!

你要多保重！

track 173

★ You have the wrong number.

你打錯電話了！

深入分析

若是你接到一通打錯電話的來電時，中文會說：「你打錯電話了！」，英文該怎麼說？不用「打」也不用"dial"，只要說："You have the wrong number."，字面意思是「你擁有錯的號碼」，卻可以充分傳達「你打錯電話！」的意思！

實用會話

A Hello? Is Jim around?

喂？吉姆在嗎？

B Jim?

吉姆？

A Is this 86473663?

這裡是86473663嗎？

B I think you have the wrong number.

我想你打錯電話了！

實用會話

A May I speak to Mr. Smith?

我要找史密斯先生聽電話。

B I think you have the wrong number.

我想你打錯電話了！

track 174

★I'm gonna be late for work.

我上班快要遲到了。

深入分析

"be late for ＋某事"是非常實用的片語，表示你快要遲到了，可能是上班、上學或和朋友的約等。

實用會話

A What's the rush?

你在趕什麼？

B I'm gonna be late for work.

我上班快要遲到了。

實用會話

A What do you want for breakfast, Jim?

吉姆，早餐想要吃什麼？

B I'm gonna be late for school. Bye, mom!

我上學快要遲到了！再見啦，媽咪！

A How about you, David?

大衛，你呢？

C Oh, I have to go, too. Bye.

喔，我也要走了，再見！

track 175

★I'm supposed to be there at noon.

我應該在中午要到那裡。

深入分析

"be supposed"表示「應該」、「預備」的意思，也是很常見的片語，帶有「我應該要…，現在卻沒有…」的意思。

實用會話

Ⓐ It's getting so late now.
現在很晚了！

Ⓑ It's still early.
還早啦！

Ⓐ I'm supposed to be there at noon.
我應該在中午要到那裡。

Ⓑ I'll call Jim and tell him you're on your way.
我會打電話給吉姆告訴他你在去的路上了！

Ⓐ Thank you so much.
真是太謝謝你了！

實用會話

Ⓐ You're supposed to be there at four.
你應該在四點鐘要到達那裡。

Ⓑ I know. Don't worry.
我知道！不用擔心！

track 176

★It's supposed to be good.

應該會不錯！

深入分析

也是和"suppose"相關的用語，同樣適用在「期望」、「認為」、「預期」的情境，此時"It's supposed to..."的句型就非常適合使用！

實用會話

Ⓐ Are there any good movies on TV?
電視有沒有播好看的電影？

Ⓑ Well, Transformers: Revenge of the Fallen is on channel 66.
嗯，66頻道有「變形金剛：復仇之戰」！

Ⓐ Oh, it's supposed to be good.
喔！應該會不錯！

Ⓑ Then why don't we watch that?
那我們何不看這部？

實用會話

Ⓐ Is it good?
這個好嗎？

Ⓑ It's supposed to be.
應該會不錯！

track 177

★What time is it?

（現在）幾點了？

深入分析

這是一句非常基本又簡單的問句，雖然沒有特別說明是要問「現在」的時間，但就可以表達「現在是幾點？」的意思。

實用會話

A What time is it?
（現在）幾點了？

B It's five to twelve.
還有五分就要十二點鐘。

A You're kidding. I'd better get ready.
真的假的？我最好趕緊準備一下！

實用會話

A Do you know what time it is?
你知道（現在）幾點了？

B It's almost ten o'clock.
快要十點鐘了！

A Oh, my God, I'm late for work.
喔，天啊！我上班要遲到了！

衍生例句

▶ What time is it now?
現在幾點了？

track 178

★What day is today?

今天是星期幾？

深入分析

很多人會將問「星期幾」和「幾月幾號」的問句搞混淆，只要記住，若是要問「星期幾？」則要用和"day"相關的片語："What day is today?"，因為每一天都是一個day。而若是要問「幾月幾號」則和「日期」有關，則用"What date is it?"

實用會話

A What day is today?

今天是星期幾？

B It's Friday.

是星期五。

實用會話

A What day is today?

今天是星期幾？

B Today is Sunday.

今天是星期天。

衍生例句

▶ What date is it?

= What's the date today?

= What's today's date?

今天是幾月幾號？

track 179

★Damn it.

可惡！

深入分析

當你發現小偷將你家裡翻箱倒櫃洗劫一空時，你一定會恨恨地說「可惡！」，英文就可以說："Damn it."或是"God damn it."

實用會話

A I was wondering if you could...

我在想你是不是可以…

B No, damn it, you wait a minute. I need to go back...

不可以，可惡！你等一下！我要回去…

A Hey! Are you listening to me?

嘿！你有在聽我說話嗎？

實用會話

A Any messages for me?

有我的留言嗎？

B No, Mr. Smith.

沒有，史密斯先生！

A God damn it. Jim said he'd give me a call.

可惡！吉姆說他會打電話給我！

track 180

★ I'll let you know.

我會讓你知道！

深入分析

當朋友向你提出邀請時，若你不確定是否能夠答應，最好的方法是告訴對方你會再告訴他你的決定：「我會再告訴你！」英文就可以說："I'll let you know."，這樣一來他就會知道你現在無法決定。但要記得，之後不論是否參加，都要通知對方喔！

實用會話

Ⓐ Are you gonna pick me up?

你有要來接我嗎？

Ⓑ I'll let you know, OK?

我會再告訴你，好嗎？

實用會話

Ⓐ Well, come with us then.

這樣喔，那就和我們一起去嘛！

Ⓑ Sure. If I'm in town, I'll call you and let you know.

好啊！如果我有在城裡，我會打電話給你，讓你知道！

track 181

★Fine with me.

我可以！

深入分析

當有人吆喝著要一起去唱KTV時，你若願意同行，除了回答："Yes, I'd to."之外，你還可以說："Fine with me."，表示「我沒問題」、「我願意」、「我可以」的意思！

實用會話

A How about having dinner with us?
要不要和我們一起去吃晚餐？

B Fine with me.
我可以！

A And you, Chuck?
查克，你呢？

C I'm not sure.
我不確定耶！

實用會話

A We probably go dancing.
我們可能會去跳舞！

B Fine with me. How about you, Jim?
我可以！吉姆，你呢？

C Don't worry about me. I'll go home.
不用擔心我！我會回家！

track 182

★A few of us are getting together.

我們一些人要聚會。

深入分析

當你要向對方說明「我們一些人」時，可以用" a few of us"，和"we"不同的是，"a few of us"是特指「一群人中的某一些人」，類似用法還有some of us、a couple of us。

實用會話

A A few of us are getting together Friday night. Do you want to join us?
我們一些人要在星期五晚上聚會。你要一起來嗎？

B Sure. I'd love to.
好啊！我很樂意！

實用會話

A Do you have any plans tomorrow?
你明天有什麼計畫嗎？

B Yes, a couple of us are heading to the pub.
有啊！我們一些人要去酒吧。

track 183

★I don't know about it.

我沒想過這個問題。

深入分析

"I don't know about it."除了可以是「我不知道這件事」之外，另一種常見的情境用法解釋為「我沒想過這個問題」，例如朋友問你是否想要出國唸書，也許「出國唸書」的想法你連奢望都不敢，你就可以回答："I don't know about it."，表示自己以前或現在都沒思考過這類的事情。

實用會話

Ⓐ Do you still want to hang out with your ex-girlfriend?

你還會想要和你的前女友出去嗎？

Ⓑ I don't know about it.

我沒想過這個問題。

Ⓐ Why not?

為什麼沒想過？

實用會話

Ⓐ What do you think of my idea?

你覺得我的主意怎麼樣？

Ⓑ I don't know about that. It may not inspire you to be a singer.

我不知道耶！可能無法激勵你成為一個歌手吧！

track 184

★I have never thought of it.

我從沒有想過這個問題！

深入分析

當對方問了你一個你從未思考的問題時，你就可以老實地告訴對方：「我想都沒有想過這個問題」，英文就可以說："I have never thought of it."，反之，若你是有思考過的，則去掉never就可以了："I have thought of it."，表示你也曾思考過相同的問題！

實用會話

A Is it possible to have our own blog?

有沒有可能我們有自己的部落格？

B I have never thought of it.

我從沒有想過這個問題！

實用會話

A I think we have to talk about it.

我覺得我們應該要談一談！

B I have thought of it.

我有想過這個問題！

track 185

★ Good luck!

祝你好運！

深入分析

祝福對方的用語"Good luck!"除了可以在對方面臨需要祝福的時刻（例如等待面試通知、考前等）獻上你的祝福，也可以當成兩人要道別說再見的情境時的道別用語。

實用會話

A I need to go now. Good-bye.

我要走囉！再見！

B OK, good luck in your test.

好吧！祝你考試有好運！

A Thanks.

謝謝！

實用會話

A I'm gonna ask her for help.

我要請她幫忙！

B Well, good luck with that.

好吧！祝你好運！

衍生例句

► Have a good day.

祝你今天順利！

track 186

★ Shut up!

閉嘴！

深入分析

這是一句非常直接的用語，當你面對的環境吵鬧不休或是一群人嘰嘰喳喳時，你都可以大聲地喝叱："Shut up!"

實用會話

A Mom, Jim took my toys.
媽，吉姆拿走我的玩具了！

B Not me, it's David.
不是我，是大衛！

C Yeap, it's David.
是啊，是大衛！

D Shut up! Go to bed now, all of you.
閉嘴！你們全部上床去睡覺！

衍生例句

► Be quiet.
安靜一點！

► Silence.
安靜點！

track 187

★ Slow down!

慢點！

深入分析

當對方匆匆忙忙、上氣不接下氣地要說話卻又說不出話來時，你就可以安撫對方："Slow down!"，凡是要讓對方慢慢來、不要急的情境下，都可以使用。

此外，若是對方開車開太快時，你也可以告誡對方："Slow down!"，表示車子開太快了，希望他減速！

實用會話

Ⓐ Jim, could you..., just come over here...
吉姆，你可以…過來這裡…嗎？

Ⓑ Slow down! What are you trying to say?
慢點！你想要說什麼？

實用會話

Ⓐ Let's hurry up. Come on.
快一點！快！

Ⓑ Slow down! It's too dangerous.
慢點！太危險了！

track 188

★Hurry up.

快一點！

深入分析

當急驚風遇見慢郎中時，一定會急得像熱鍋上的螞蟻吧，此時就可以提醒對方："Hurry up."，舉凡是對方動作太慢、說話吞吞吐吐的情境下都適用，例如對方對是要喝咖啡或果汁一直遲遲無法做出決定時，你就催促："Hurry up."，讓對方知道你可是已經有點不耐煩了喔！

實用會話

A Shall we?

要走了嗎？

B Not yet. I'm not ready.

還沒！我還沒準備好！

A Hurry up, OK?

快一點，好嗎？

實用會話

A Let's hurry up.

快一點啦！

B But I don't wanna go with you...

可是我不想和你一起去耶…

track 189

★ Me, too.

我也是！

深入分析

當你要附和對方的想法、觀念、決定時，中文會說「我也是！」，英文就只要說："Me too."，但是請記住，這個"Me, too."的用法只適合在「肯定句」情境下的，若是否定句的附和，則有其他說法。

實用會話

A I'm so hungry.

我好餓喔！

B Me, too.

我也是！

實用會話

A I'm feeling very sleepy.

我好想睡喔！

B Me, too.

我也是！

實用會話

A I want to go to the store.

我要去商店。

B Me, too.

我也是！

track 190

★ So do I.

我也一樣。

深入分析

在肯定句的附和情境中，除了"Me, too."之外，你也可以用"so＋助動詞＋主詞"的句型表示，例如對方說："I saw David last night."，你就可以附和說："So did I."，要注意的是，助動詞的時態要和對方所說的句子相同。

實用會話

Ⓐ I hate traveling all the way to Scotland by train.

我討厭搭火車旅遊蘇格蘭。

Ⓑ So do I.

我也一樣（討厭）。

實用會話

Ⓐ I failed my math exam.

我數學考試搞砸了！

Ⓑ You, too? So did I!

你也是？我也一樣（搞砸了）。

實用會話

Ⓐ We stayed at the Four Seasons Hotel in Seattle.

我們住宿在西雅圖的四季飯店。

B What a coincidence! So did we.

好巧！我們也是！

徹底學會英文

So will I.

我也是！

這種「我也是」的附和句子，最主要就是「助動詞」前後一致的原則，例如對方所說的句子是未來式，例如有will的句子，你同樣要用未來式表示。

A：I think I'll go to bed.

我想我最好上床睡覺！

B：So will I.

我也是！

A：I've met Bill Clinton.

我有遇到Bill Clinton。

B：So have I.

我也是！

A：I was very upset by the news.

聽見這個消息我們難過！

B：So was I.

我也是！

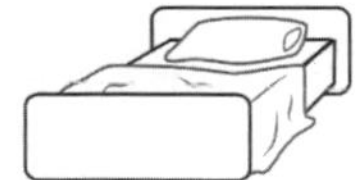

track 191

★ Me neither.

我也不。

深入分析

在附和的情境中，若對方所說的句子是屬於「否定式」的句子，亦即有"not"的單字出現，則你的附和句子就要用"neither"表示。值得注意的是，動詞的時態也要一致。

實用會話

A I don't want to go fishing this afternoon.

今天下午我不想去釣魚！

B Me neither.

我也不想去。

實用會話

A I'd never go there alone at night.

我從不會在晚上的時候自己去。

B Me neither.

我也不會！

實用會話

A I don't feel like going out tonight.

我今天晚上不想出去！

B Me neither.

我也不想！

track 192

★ Take it easy.

別緊張！

深入分析

若是對方緊張兮兮或是情緒很激動時，你除了安撫對方說："Calm down."之外，你還可以說："Take it easy."，表示「放輕鬆」、「別緊張」的意思，"easy"有輕鬆、舒適的意思。

實用會話

A I'm so nervous.

我好緊張！

B Take it easy.

別緊張！

實用會話

A How do I look, Jim?

吉姆，我看起來怎麼樣？

B Take it easy. You look beautiful.

別緊張！你看起來很漂亮。

衍生例句

▶ Calm down.

冷靜一下！

▶ Relax.

放輕鬆！

track 193

★ Are you going out with Jim?

你今天晚上要和吉姆出去嗎？

深入分析

"go out"是常用片語，是指「出去」的意思，至於出去做什麼？可以解釋的原因非常多，可以是因為約會、碰面、出去逛逛、消磨時間等，但很多時候是解釋兩人正在交往的意思。類似這種語焉不詳的用法還包含："hang out"。

實用會話

A Are you going out with Jim tonight?

你今天晚上要和吉姆出去嗎？

B Uh-huh, I'm supposed to meet him at five.

嗯哼，我和他五點鐘要碰面。

實用會話

A How long have you been going out with him?

你和他交往多久了？

B About 3 months.

大概三個月！

實用會話

A Do you want to hang out tonight?

今晚要出來到處逛逛嗎？

B I'd love to.

好啊！

徹底學會英文

Are you seeing someone?
你有交往的對象嗎？

可別以為"Are you seeing someone?"是說「你正在看某人嗎？」這種字面意思是很容易讓人產生誤解的，這是一句非常道地的英文，表示問對方「你有交往的對象嗎？」

A：Are you seeing someone now?
你現在有交往的對象嗎？

B：I don't wanna talk about it right now.
我現在不想討論這件事！

track 194

★I haven't made up my mind.

我還沒有決定！

深入分析

"make up one's mind"是常用片語，表示「某人做出決定」的意思，例如餐廳侍者問你是否要點餐了（Are you ready to order?），你卻還在考慮要哪一個主餐（或甜點）時，就可以對侍者說："I haven't made up my mind."

實用會話

Ⓐ What's your plan?

你的計畫是什麼？

Ⓑ I have no idea. I haven't made up my mind.

我不知道！我還沒有決定！

實用會話

Ⓐ Where are you going?

你們要去哪裡？

Ⓑ We haven't made up our minds yet.

我們還沒有決定！

track 195

★ Maybe we will.

也許我們會！

深入分析

當對方提議某件事，你不但願意嘗試，又或者未來你有機會這麼做時，就可以告訴對方："Maybe I will."。因為是表示「未來的可能性」，所以是用未來式will的句型，通常也可以在will後面接原形動詞，以完整表達句子。

實用會話

A Why don't you go to see a movie? How about The Curious Case of Benjamin Button?

你們何不去看電影？要不要看「班傑明的奇幻旅程」？

B Sounds great. Maybe we will.

聽起來不錯！也許我們會去！

實用會話

A What are you gonna do about it?

你要怎麼處理這件事？

B Nothing. Maybe I'll keep it that way.

什麼都不做！也許我會保持這個樣子！

---

track 196

★ Thank you very much.

非常謝謝你！

深入分析

若是要「感謝」對方，中文就只要說「謝謝」或「太感激你了！」，英文中最常見的用法就是："Thank you."，若是要表達更深層的謝意，則可以說："Thank you very much." 或是"Thank you so much."

此外，若是要傳達中文的「多謝啦！」則可以說："Thanks a lot."

實用會話

A Where is the post office?

郵局在哪裡？

B It's over there. Next to the bank.

就在那裡！在銀行旁邊。

A I see. Thank you very much.

我瞭解了！非常謝謝你！

實用會話

A Let me help you with it.

我來幫你！

B Thank you so much.

真是太謝謝你了！

track 197

★Thank you for your advice.

謝謝你的建議。

深入分析

道謝的原因有很多種，要特別說明「為了…（某事）謝謝你」就可以利用"Thank you for..."的句型，for後面加道謝的原因，例如若是要針對對方所提供的建議，則可以說："Thank you for your advice."（ 謝謝你的建議。）

實用會話

Ⓐ That's it. That's what you have to do now.

就這樣！你就該這麼做！

Ⓑ Sounds great. Thank you for your advice.

聽起來不錯！謝謝你的建議。

實用會話

Ⓐ Here you are.

我來（幫你）！

Ⓑ Oh, thank you for your help.

喔，謝謝你的幫忙！

Ⓐ You're welcome.

不客氣！

track 198

★ Thanks for asking.

還是謝謝你的邀請。

深入分析

若是對方對你提出邀請，而你必須拒絕時，記得在最後要謝謝對方的邀請，這是一種禮貌，英文就可以說："Thanks for asking."，句中的"asking"是指「邀請」的意思。

實用會話

A David! What are you doing here?

大衛？你在這裡做什麼？

B I'm waiting for you. Say, would you like to go to Jim's party with me?

我正在等你！是這樣的，你要和我一起去參加吉姆的派對嗎？

A I'd love to but I can't. Sorry.

我很想去，可是我無法去耶！抱歉！

B It's OK.

沒關係！

A Thanks for asking.

還是謝謝你的邀請。

實用會話

A I was wondering, would you like to go to the prom with me next week?

我在想你下星期要不要和我去參加舞會？

B Well, I really don't think I can. I have other plans. Thanks for asking, though.

我想我真得沒辦法去，我有另外的計畫，不過還是謝謝你的邀請。

A That's O.K. Maybe some other time.

沒關係！以後還有機會！

track 199

★As soon as possible!

越快越好！

深入分析

若是對方問你「期限是什麼時候」，而你希望對方能盡快完成時，就只要說："As soon as possible!"，字面意思是「盡你所能地快一點」，也就是「越快越好！」的意思。

此外，"as soon as possible"也可以放在句尾，用以補充整個句子。

實用會話

A Do me a favor. Please type this letter for me.
幫我個忙！幫我打這封信！

B OK. When do you want this?
好！你什麼時候要？

A As soon as possible!
越快越好！

實用會話

A You need to repair the door as soon as possible.
你最好趕緊修好門！

B Why me? I'm in the middle of something.
為什麼是我？我正在忙耶！

track 200

★ Be careful!

當心點！

深入分析

若是一位步履闌珊的老人家要穿越穿流不息的馬路時，大家一定會為他捏一把冷汗，此時你就應該發揮愛心扶老人家穿越馬路，順便提醒對方："Be careful!"，這是一句原形動詞在句首的提醒用語。

實用會話

Ⓐ Oh, my God, what is that?

喔，天啊！這是什麼？

Ⓑ Be careful! It's so dangerous here.

當心點！這裡很危險！

實用會話

Ⓐ Did you see that?

你有看見那個嗎？

Ⓑ Be careful. You're asking for big trouble.

當心點！你是自找麻煩！

實用會話

Ⓐ Be careful to look both ways when you cross the street.

過馬路的時候要小心兩側的方向。

Ⓑ We will, mom.

我們會的，媽咪！

徹底學會英文

Watch out!

小心點！

「小心點！」也可以用："watch out"表示，但可別以為"watch out"是「往外看」的意思喔，而是提醒對方「小心」、「注意」的意思。此外，類似的用法還有"look out"。

A：Hey, watch out.
嘿，小心點！

B：Oh, thanks. I didn't see that.
喔，謝謝！我沒看到！

A：Look out! It's a trap.
小心！是個陷阱！

B：What trap? I saw nothing.
什麼陷阱？我什麼都沒看見啊！

track 201

★ Onion, please.

我要點洋蔥，謝謝！

深入分析

這種"名詞，+ please"的句型，最適合在回答對方詢問你要何種選擇時使用，例如主人端出咖啡請你喝時，可能會問你："How many?"（喝咖啡要加幾顆糖？），你就可以簡單地說："One, please."，表示你只要加一顆糖的意思，是非常簡單的一句回答短語。

實用會話

A I think I'll have soup. What kinds do you have?

我想要點湯！你們有什麼湯？

B Onion and pea soup. Which one do you like?

洋蔥湯和豆子湯。你要哪一種？

A Onion, please.

我要點洋蔥（湯），謝謝！

實用會話

A What do you want to drink? Coffee or tea?

你想喝什麼？咖啡還是茶？

A Coffee, please.

請給我咖啡，謝謝！

徹底學會英文

No, thanks.

不用了，謝謝！

相較於上述回答你所下的決定用語，若你的回答是屬於「不用」或「我不要」等否定情境，則可以回答："No, thanks."，表示「我不用，謝謝！」

A：How about you, sir?

先生，您呢？

B：No, thanks.

不用了，謝謝！

A：What would you like to drink?
　你想喝點什麼？
B：No, thanks.
　不用了，謝謝！

track 202

★Which way is the post office?

到郵局要走哪條路？

深入分析

當你迷路時，應該先找某個你熟悉地點，好讓你可以辨識自己所在的方位，例如你可以問："Which way is the nearest MRT?"，表示「最近的捷運站要走哪條路？」最常用的句型為 "Which way is＋地點?"

實用會話

Ⓐ Excuse me. Which way is the post office?
請問一下，到郵局要走哪條路？

Ⓑ That way.
往那個方向！

Ⓐ Thank you very much.
非常謝謝你！

實用會話

Ⓐ Which way is the museum?
博物館怎麼走？

B Sorry, I'm a stranger here myself.

抱歉，我對這裡也不熟！

track 203

★We're looking for a place to have lunch.

我們要找個地方吃午餐。

深入分析

在這個句子中，有兩個重要的片語，第一個是"look for + sth./sb."表示「尋找…」、「尋求…」的意思，例如："I'm looking for my missing kid."（我正在尋找我失蹤的孩子）。

第二，"have ＋ 餐點"，這裡可不是「擁有餐點」的意思，而是指「吃餐點」。

實用會話

A May I help you?

需要我幫忙嗎？

B Yes, we're looking for a place to have lunch.

是的！我們要找個地方吃午餐。

實用會話

A What can I do for you?

有什麼需要我協助的嗎？

Ⓑ I'm looking for a place to stay.
我要找個地方過夜。

---

track 204

★ That's all I need.

我就要這些。

深入分析

當你要表明「這些就是全部我所需要的」時，就可以說"That's all I need."，這是一種結束挑選或是完成目的後的用語。

實用會話

Ⓐ May I help you?
需要我幫忙嗎？

Ⓑ Yes. I want five beef steaks and two pounds of pork.
是的！我想要買五塊牛排和兩磅的豬肉。

Ⓐ OK. Anything else?
好的！還需要其他東西嗎？

Ⓑ No. That's all I need.
沒有了！我就要這些。

Ⓐ No problem, sir.
好的，先生。

徹底學會英文

That's all.
全部就這些！

另一種類似「就是這些」的說法則為"That's all."，表示「就這樣！」或是「全部就這些！」的意思。

A：Here you are.
給你！

B：Is that all? Are you sure?
就這樣？你確定嗎？

A：Anything else?
還需要其他東西嗎？

B：No, that's all.
不用！全部就這些！

track 205

★ Here comes my bus.

我等的公車來了。

深入分析

"Here comes..."有多好用？例如你等的公車來了，就可以說："Here comes my bus."，或是表達「剛好走過來的是大衛」的情境時，就只要簡單地說："Here comes David."，注意，come要用單數形式comes表示。

實用會話

Ⓐ Maybe this is good for you.
也許這對你來說是好事。

Ⓑ I realize that. Oh, here comes my bus. Bye.
我明白！喔，我等的公車來了。再見！

Ⓐ Good-bye.
再見！

實用會話

Ⓐ Look! Here comes Eric.
你看！是艾瑞克耶！

Ⓑ Why don't you ask him for his help?
你何不找他幫？

Ⓐ I will.
我會的！

track 206

★I have to catch a plane.

我要趕搭飛機。

深入分析

"catch＋交通工具"的字面意思是「追趕交通工具」，也就是「趕著要去搭乘某個交通工具」的意思，例如"catch a train"（趕搭火車），或是 "catch the 10:30 plane"（趕搭十點卅分的飛機）。

實用會話

Ⓐ What' the rush, Alex?

艾利斯，你在趕什麼？

Ⓑ I have to catch a plane.

我要趕搭飛機。

實用會話

Ⓐ I have to catch the 6:05 train.

我要趕搭六點五分的火車。

Ⓑ It's five thirty now.

現在五點半了！

Ⓐ I'd better get going soon.

我最好趕緊走！

衍生例句

▶ I just caught the plane.

我剛好趕上了飛機。

track 207

★ Time is running out.

沒時間了。

深入分析

"run out"表示「用罄」、「耗盡」或「不足」的意思，包含「時間」、「汽油」、「金錢」、「食物」…等均適用，例如對顧客說某項商品賣完了，就可以說"run out"。

實用會話

Ⓐ It's almost seven o'clock.

快要七點鐘了！

Ⓑ My God. Time is running out.

我的天啊！沒時間了！

實用會話

Ⓐ Have you got any milk?

你們還有牛奶嗎？

Ⓑ Sorry, I've run out.

抱歉，賣完囉！

徹底學會英文

Time is up.
時間到囉！

和「時間不夠」（Time is running out.）很類似的另一種說法是「時間快到了」，英文可以說："Time is up."，強調「截止的時間快到了」的意思。

A：Time is up!
時間到囉！

B：Five more minutes, please.
拜託再給我五分鐘！

track 208

★ Well done!

幹得好！

深入分析

當你要稱讚對方表現良好時，中文會說「幹得好！」，英文就可以說："Well done!" 或是"Good job."，例如部屬加班很多天終於完成報告時，你就可以拍拍對方的肩膀，告訴他："Well done!"

實用會話

Ⓐ Well done!

幹得好！

Ⓑ You really think so?

你真的這麼認為？

Ⓐ Of course. You're always doing a good job!

當然！你總是表現得很出色！

實用會話

Ⓐ Come on, I want to show you something.

快來，我要給你看個東西！

Ⓑ Wow! Well done!

哇！幹得好！

衍生例句

► Good job!

做得好！

track 209

★ Do me a favor, OK?

幫個忙，好嗎？

深入分析

"do someone a favor"是常用片語，表示「幫助某人」的意思，你可以說："Please do me a favor."（請幫我一個忙！），另一種用法是："Would you do me a favor?"（可以幫我一個忙嗎？）

實用會話

A Do me a favor, OK?
幫個忙，好嗎？

B Sure. What is it?
好啊！什麼事？

A Would you give this note to Sandy for me?
可以幫我把這張紙條給珊蒂嗎？

實用會話

A Would you do me a favor?
可以幫我一個忙嗎？

B Of course.
當然好！

A Please call a cab for me.
幫我叫一輛計程車。

B No problem.
沒問題！

徹底學會英文

Give me a hand.
幫某人一個忙！

大部分的人都知道"hand"是「手」意思，而中文的「協助」有用「好幫手」 表示，在英文中也有相對應說法："give someone a hand"。在羅賓威廉斯主演的電影「虎克船長」中，有一幕戲虎克船長說了一句："Give me a hand!"，不知哪個烏龍船員居然丟了一隻手給船長，你可別犯了同樣的錯誤喔，這句話可是「請幫我一個忙」的意思。

此外，同樣的情境也可以說用："need a hand"表示。

A：Could you give me a hand with the table, please?
可以請你幫我搬這張桌子嗎？

B：I'd be glad to.
好啊！

A：I think Eric might need a hand with his homework.
我想艾瑞克需要有人幫他做功課！

B：Are you crazy?
你瘋啦？

A：No. I'm trying to help him.
沒有啊！我只是想要幫他啊！

track 210

★ Tell her I'll call her back after 3.

告訴她我三點鐘之後會回電話給她。

深入分析

若是你希望對方能幫你留言：「請『轉告』某人…」，英文該怎麼說？可別急著查字典找「轉告」的用法，一般來說可以用tell的用法："tell someone..."，例如「轉告他我會準時回來」，英文就可以說："Tell him I'll be back on time."。

實用會話

Ⓐ What do you want me to tell her?

你要我告訴她什麼事？

Ⓑ Tell her I'll call her back after 3.

告訴她我三點鐘之後會回電話給她。

實用會話

Ⓐ May I leave a message?

我可以留言嗎？

Ⓑ Sure. What is it?

好啊！是什麼？

Ⓐ Tell Sandy I'll come back at 4.

告訴珊蒂，我會在四點鐘回來！

track 211

★Do you mind?

你介意嗎？

深入分析

現在許多公共場所都禁菸，所以當你想要吞雲吐霧一番時，應該先問問周遭的人，此時你的肢體動作應該是拿出香菸作勢要抽，並問："Do you mind?"，表示「你介意（我抽菸）嗎？」

舉凡你的任何行為，只要你想要得到對方允許、同意，"Do you mind?"都適用。

實用會話

Ⓐ Do you mind?

你介意嗎？

Ⓑ No, not at all.

不，一點都不會的！

實用會話

Ⓐ Do you mind if I smoke?

你介意我抽煙嗎？

Ⓑ No, I don't mind.

不，我不介意！

實用會話

Ⓐ Do you mind if I open the window?

你介意我開窗嗎？

Ⓑ Yes, I do mind.

是的，我介意！

track 212

★Do I have to?

非這麼做不可嗎？

深入分析

"have to"是常用片語，表示「必須」的意思，例如當你心不甘情不願地被迫做某一件事時，你仍可以利用最後的一點希望問問對方："Do I have to?"，表示「我非得這麼做不可嗎？」

此外，to的後面可以加原形動詞，表示「必須去做某事」的意思，例如「我必須要去接我的女朋友」英文就可以說："I have to pick up my girlfriend."

實用會話

A Do I have to?

非這麼做不可嗎？

B You heard me.

你有聽到我說的話了！

實用會話

A You should study more.

你應該要多用功一點！

B Do I have to?

非這麼做不可嗎？

A Yes, you should.

是的，你是應該要！

track 213

★ What a pity!

太遺憾了！

深入分析

本來朋友答應你要一起去參加舞會的，但是他臨時生病，所以不能和你一起去，你就可以說：" What a pity!"，這種"what..."的句型，非常適合使用在敘述某一件「非常…」的事件中，例如：" What an adorable kid."（這小孩真可愛！）、"What lovely weather."（天氣真好！）

實用會話

Ⓐ Hello?

喂？

Ⓑ Hi, Jim. This is Karen.

嗨，吉姆，我是凱倫。

Ⓐ What's up, Karen?

有事嗎，凱倫？

Ⓑ I must be getting a cold. I'm afraid I couldn't make it tonight.

我一定是感冒了！我今晚可能無法過去了！

Ⓐ What a pity! Did you go to see a doctor?

太遺憾了！妳有去看醫生嗎？

Ⓑ Yes, I did.

有啊，我有去！

track 214

★What do you think?

你怎麼認為？

深入分析

當你要詢問對方的想法或意見時，就非常適合使用這句："What do you think?"，若要特指「對這一件事的意見」，則也可以說："What do you think about it?"

實用會話

A Look at the crowd. What do you think?

你看那個人潮！你怎麼認為？

B That must be a great place to eat.

這一定是一間不錯的餐廳！

實用會話

A What do you think? Isn't it good?

你怎麼認為？不好嗎？

B Well, I can't make up my mind.

嗯，我無法下決定耶！

衍生例句

▶ What's your opinion?

你的想法呢？

track 215

★ Believe it or not!

信不信由你！

深入分析

若是對方質疑你的論點或想法，你就可以回嗆對方："Believe it or not!"，表示「信不信由你！」，有點類似中文口語情境中的「隨便你相不相信」！

實用會話

A I don't think she would do this to me.
我不認為她會這麼對我！

B Fine. Believe it or not!
隨便！信不信由你！

實用會話

A Believe it or not! This is delicious.
信不信由你！真的很好吃！

B You really think so?
你真的這麼認為？

track 216

★ You're unbelievable.

你真是令人感到訝異！

深入分析

表示對方的言行讓你感到不相信，或是感到不可思議時，都可以說："You're unbelievable."，也帶有一點"I can't believe it."（我真是不敢相信）的味道！

實用會話

A You're good. That's so funny.

你真行！真是有趣！

B Look at you. You're unbelievable.

瞧瞧你！你真是令人感到訝異！

C Hey, I just did what Mr. Jones told me to do.

嘿，我只是照瓊斯先生叫我做的事去做啊！

衍生例句

▶ Unbelievable.

= It's unbelievable.

這件事真是令人不敢相信。

track 217

★ Are you sure?

你確定嗎？

深入分析

當你不確定對方所說的話時，就可以說："Are you sure?"，有點類似說明「是我沒聽清楚還是你說錯了？」的探詢意味。

另一種確認的完整說法則是："Are you sure about that?"，表示「那件事你有確定嗎？」特指"about that"(那件事)。

實用會話

Ⓐ When are you coming back?
你什麼時候要回來？

Ⓑ This Friday night at six.
這個星期五晚上六點鐘。

Ⓐ Are you sure?
你確定嗎？

實用會話

Ⓐ Are you sure about that?
那件事你確定嗎？

Ⓑ Yes, I am. Why?
是啊，我有確定！為什麼這麼問？

track 218

★I'll take the bus.

我會搭公車。

深入分析

「搭車」的英文怎麼說？很簡單，只要用"take"就可以完全搞定「搭公車」，例如，你可以說："I'll take the bus to New York."（我要搭公車去紐約），而搭火車則叫做"take the train"。

實用會話

A How are you getting there?

你要怎麼過去那裡？

B I'll take the bus.

我會搭公車。

A Well, listen, if you need a ride to the airport, let me know.

是喔，聽好！如果你要我順便載你過去機場，就告訴我一聲。

B Oh, thanks. That's very nice of you.

喔，謝啦！你真是好心！

track 219

★ Any day will do.

哪一天都行！

深入分析

當對方問你「哪一天適合？」時，你就可以很隨性地說：「哪一天都行！」，表示你的時間是很有彈性、很自由的。對方可能會用這樣的句型問你："When do you want...?"（你想要什麼時候…？）英文就可以回答："Any day will do."

實用會話

A Why don't you come over for dinner?
你何不過來吃晚餐？

B I'd love to. When do you want me to come?
我很願意啊！你要我哪一天過去？

A Any day will do.
哪一天都行。

B Well, how about this Friday night?
那這個星期五晚上呢？

A Sounds great.
聽起來不錯耶！

track 220

★ Any time.

不客氣！

深入分析

「不客氣！」的英文很多人都知道叫做"You're welcome."，現在教你另一種常見的美式用法，叫做："Any time."，例如對方臨下車時，謝謝你讓他搭順風車，如果是你很熟識、常見面的朋友，你就可以說："Any time."，表示「隨時歡迎你（搭便車）」的意思。

但若是陌生人的"thumb a ride"，則你只要在對方說道謝時回應"You're welcome."就可以，因為你再提供便車讓他搭的機會應該很小，所以此時的情境就不必說："Any time."

實用會話

Ⓐ Thank you for your help.

謝謝你的幫忙！

Ⓑ Any time.

不客氣！

實用會話

Ⓐ Oh, by the way, I really appreciate your ride.

喔，對了，我真的很感謝你讓我搭便車！

Ⓑ Any time.

不客氣！

track 221

★After you.

您先請。

深入分析

美國人也注重禮儀，像是進出門口、電梯等，都會幫後面的人扶著門，而若是面對婦孺時，也會先說："After you."，也就是中文的「您先請」。

此外，"After you."也曾經在電影史瑞克 2 中出現，場景是在史瑞克告訴薑餅人"After you."，表示「由你先進攻」、「看你的了」的意思。

實用會話

A You first.

您請。

B After you.

您先請。

A Thanks.

謝謝！

實用會話

A After you, Mrs. Smith.

史密斯太太，您先請。

B Thank you so much.

真是太謝謝你了！

衍生例句

▶ Ladies first.

女士優先！

track 222

★Come on.

趕快！

深入分析

要催促慢吞吞的孩子動作快一點，你就可以說："Come on."，表示「快一點！」而若是大家要一起出門時，你也可以說："Come on."，表示「我們走吧！」

此外，"Oh, come on."則表示「你少來了！」、「別開我玩笑了！」

實用會話

Ⓐ Wait for me.

等等我！

Ⓑ Come on. It's too late.

趕快！太晚了！

實用會話

Ⓐ Come on. Let's go.

來吧！ 我們走吧！

Ⓑ But I really don't feel well.

可是我真的覺得不舒服耶！

實用會話

Ⓐ You haven't changed a bit.

你一點都沒改變耶！

Ⓑ Oh, come on now. I used to have more hair, didn't I?

喔，別這樣說啦！我以前頭髮比較多，對吧？

track 223

★Do I make myself clear?

我說得夠清楚了嗎？

深入分析

當對方企圖質疑你時，你可以以自己的權威或背景，告訴對方："Do I make myself clear?"，意思是「我說的話很清楚了，你聽懂我的意思了嗎？」

實用會話

A Do I make myself clear?
我說得夠清楚了嗎？

B Yes, but I don't wanna...
是很清楚，但是我不想…

A I thought you wanted my advice.
我以為你想要聽聽我的建議！

B Whatever. You'll see the light, eventually.
不管了！你最後會瞭解的！

實用會話

A Remember to finish your assignment by this Friday. Do I make myself clear?
記得要在本週五之前完成你的功課！我說得夠清楚了嗎？

B Yes, Mrs. Jones.
是的，瓊斯女士！

track 224

★I have something to tell you.

我有事要告訴你。

深入分析

當你有事要告訴對方時，就會說「我有事要告訴你」，這句話英文的說法幾乎和中文一模一樣，就叫做"I have something to tell you."

另一種想和對方交談的用語，則可以用"I need to talk to you."，表示「我要和你聊一聊」。

實用會話

Ⓐ Jim? I have something to tell you.
吉姆？我有事要告訴你。

Ⓑ What?
有什麼事？

實用會話

Ⓐ I need to talk to you.
我要和你聊一聊！

Ⓑ Sure. Come on in.
好啊！進來吧！

衍生例句

▶ Got a minute to talk?
現在有空談一談嗎？

▶ Do you have a moment?
你有空嗎？

track 225

★I quit!

我不幹了！

深入分析

當你要離職時，你可以說："I quit!"，而若是對於大家本來協議要一起完成的事，你如今表明「退出」、「不幹了」，也非常適合直接說："I quit!"

實用會話

A I'm not sure I can do it.
恐怕這事我幹不了。

B How dare you.
你敢？

A Why not? I quit!
為什麼不敢！我不幹了！

B You come back here. Did you hear me?
你給我回來這裡！你有聽到嗎？

實用會話

A Come on, buddy.
兄弟，走吧！

B I quit!
我不幹了！

A You what?
你說什麼？

track 226

★I have no choice.

我別無選擇。

深入分析

當被迫做出某個選擇或決定時，就可以無奈地說："I have no choice."，同樣的情境也可以說："I don't have a choice."，表示你「不得不」的處境。

實用會話

A I have no choice.
我別無選擇。

B What do you mean you have no choice?
你是什麼意思你別無選擇？

A I can't leave him alone out there.
我不能把他一個人丟在那裡！

實用會話

A Why? Why did you call her?
為什麼？你為什麼要打電話給她？

B I don't have a choice.
我別無選擇。

A Yes, you do.
有的，你可以有選擇！

衍生例句

► I can't help it.
我情不自禁！

track 227

★I'm here on vacation.

我是來這裡度假的！

深入分析

當你在異地遇到熟識的人時，對方可能會問你：「什麼風把你吹來這裡？」（What brings you here?），若你是來度假的，就可以說："I'm here on vacation."，或是"I'm here on business."（我是來這裡出差的！）

實用會話

A What brings you to New York?
你怎麼會來紐約？

B I'm here on vacation. You, too?
我是來這裡度假的！你也是嗎？

A No, I live here.
不是！我住在這裡！

B You're kidding. How long have you been living here?
真的假的？你住在這裡多久了？

A For three years.
有五年了！

track 228

★What's the rush?

你在趕什麼？

深入分析

當你看見有人好像匆匆忙忙時，就可以問他："What's the rush?"，表示「你在趕什麼？」或「你趕著要去哪裡？」的意思！此外，"What the rush?"也可以有反問意味：「有什麼好急的？慢慢來就可以啦！」

實用會話

Ⓐ What's the rush?

你在趕什麼？

Ⓑ I'm late for work.

我上班要遲到了！

實用會話

Ⓐ Hey, you should clean your room now.

嘿，現在你應該要整理你的房間啦！

Ⓑ What's the rush? I've got all day.

有什麼好急的？我有一整天的時間

track 229

★It's hard to tell.

很難說！

深入分析

當你不認同對方所下的結論時，你除了可以說："I don't think so."之外，你也可以說："It's hard to tell."，表示「很難說！」也是暗示對方不要妄下定論的意思。

實用會話

A What do you think?

你的看法呢？

B I don't think she is right.

我認為她是不對的。

A It's hard to tell.

很難說！

B What do you mean by that?

你這是什麼意思？

徹底學會英文

How can you tell?

你怎麼分辨得出來？

一般說來"tell"是指「說話」的意思，但是在某些時候也有「分辨」的解釋，多半要用前後文來判斷是哪一種解釋，以"How can you tell?"為例，若解釋「你怎麼能說」也沒有錯，但很多時候是指「你怎麼能分辨得出來？」

A：He's Dutch.
他是荷蘭人。
B：How can you tell?
你怎麼分辨得出來？

A：How can you tell the difference?
你怎麼分辨得出來不同？
B：I just know it.
我就是知道！

track 230

★ Don't count on me.

別指望我。

深入分析

當對方殷切期盼你的協助，而你卻不這麼認為時，你就可以直接告訴對方放棄這個想法："Don't count on me."，表示「別指望我」的意思。"count on someone"是指「仰賴某人」的意思。

實用會話

A Can anyone pick it up for me?
有誰可以幫我撿起來嗎？

B Don't count on me.
別指望我。

實用會話

A Did you send the report to Jim?
你有寄報告給吉姆嗎？

B Yes. I did. And I also typed the letter for you. It's on your desk.

有的，我有寄！我還把信打好字了，在你的桌上！

A Thanks. I know I can always count on you.

謝啦！我就知道我可以依賴你！

track 231

★Not anymore.

不再是了！

深入分析

表示以前是如此，但從現在開始，卻不再和先前一樣時，都可以說："Not anymore."

另一種延伸用法，則是"not... anymore"片語，適合在否定句中使用，例如："We're not friends anymore."，表示「我們絕交了」的意思！

實用會話

A He picks on people. I hate him.

他老是批評人！我討厭他！

B Hey, he's your friend.

嘿，他是你的朋友啊！

A Not anymore.

不再是了！

實用會話

Ⓐ Do you still love this guy?
你還愛這傢伙嗎？

Ⓑ Not anymore.
不再是了！

Ⓐ I hope so.
希望是如此！

track 232

★ It's over now.

現在事情都結束了！

深入分析

電影中常出現的情節：在經歷了許多事件後，男主角花了好大的功夫才救出被綁架的女主角，此時男主角一定會說的一句話是："It's over now."，表示「你現在安全了」、「一切都過去了」的意思！

實用會話

Ⓐ Help me out, dad.
老爸，救我出去！

Ⓑ I'm here. It's over now.
我在這裡！現在事情都結束了！

實用會話

A Wake up, Sandy.

珊蒂，醒一醒！

B I had a nightmare.

我做了個惡夢！

A I'm here with you. It's all over now.

我就在這裡陪妳！現在事情都結束了！

---

track 233

★I hope so.

希望如此。

深入分析

當對方下了個結論後，你便隨即附和對方的言論時，就可以說："I hope so."，例如老弟告訴你他可以在十天之內減重5公斤，你就可說："I hope so."

此外，"I hope so."有的時候也有看笑話或不認為對方辦得到的意味。

實用會話

A I can get what I want.

我能得到我想要的。

B I hope so.

希望如此。

實用會話

Ⓐ Maybe you're right. I'd try again.

也許你是對的！我會再試一次！

Ⓑ I hope so.

希望如此。

衍生例句

► I suppose so.

我也這麼認為。

track 234

★I have been told.

我已經被告知了。

深入分析

當你要告訴對方：「有人告訴我這件事」時，就可以說："I have been told."，表示「我已經知道了，而且是由其他人告訴我的！」

實用會話

Ⓐ You know what? I'm on a diet.

你知道嗎？我在節食。

Ⓑ Sure. I have been told.

當然，我已經被告知了。

徹底學會英文

I told you so.
我告訴過你啦！

當事前已經告知對方某件事，但對方仍舊執意自己的想法，後來卻後悔時，你就可以說："I told you so."，表示「我告訴過你啦！」雖然有點馬後砲，但可以讓對方知道「這是你不聽我的話的結果」，有一點苛責對方的意味。

A：I shouldn't come back here.
我實在不應該回來這裡的！

B：I told you so.
我告訴過你啦！

track 235

★I heard about that.

我聽說了。

深入分析

另一種和"I've been told"類似用法是："I heard about that."，強調「消息」，表示「我已經聽說這件事了！」"hear about..."是常用片語，表示「聽說某事」的意思。

實用會話

A I broke up with David.
我和大衛分手了！

B I heard about that. What happened to you two?

我聽說了。你們兩個人怎麼回事？

實用會話

A I've decided to go home.

我已經決定要回家了！

B I heard about that. When?

我聽說了。什麼時候？

A Next week.

就在下星期！

track 236

★ You'll never find out.

你永遠不會知道的！

深入分析

"find out"是常見的動詞片語，表示「察覺」、「得知」的意思，特別是針對真相或亟欲知道的事等，例如："I'm gonna find out what happened."（我要去查一查發生了什麼事！）而"You'll never find out."則是相反意思，表示「永遠都不會知道的」，表示「真相將石沈大海」，或是「永遠沒有機會」的意思，這種情境用法通常用未來式表示。

實用會話

A What happened to her?

她發生了什麼事了？

B You'll never find out.

你永遠不會知道的！

實用會話

A Maybe we should go back to finish it. What do you think?

也許我們應該回頭去完成！你覺得的呢？

B We'll never find out.

我們永遠不會知道的！

track 237

★ Here you are.

給你。

深入分析

要拿某個物品給對方時，中文會說：「給你」，英文就可以說："Here you are."，例如你搭計程車要拿車資給計程車司機時，就可以說："Here you are."，表示「東西在這裡，你拿去吧」的意思。

實用會話

A Here you are.

給你。

Ⓑ What is it?

這是什麼？

Ⓐ I don't know. David left it for you.

我不知道！大衛留給你的！

實用會話

Ⓐ Sugar?

要加糖嗎？

Ⓑ Yes, please.

好的，謝謝你！

Ⓐ Here you are.

給你。

track 238

★ Hold on.

等一等。

深入分析

當你希望對方能「稍候片刻」時，就可以說："Hold on."，例如秘書接到找老闆的來電時，要轉接電話前，就可以告訴來電者："Hold on."，也可以用客氣一點的語氣說："Hold on a second, please."

實用會話

Ⓐ Hold on. I'll be right back.

等一等。我馬上回來！

B Come back! Don't leave me alone.

你回來啦！不要把我一個人丟在這裡！

實用會話

A May I know who's speaking?

請問您大名？

B This is John Jackson.

我是約翰・傑森。

A Mr. Jackson, please hold on a second.

傑森先生，請稍候片刻。

衍生例句

▶ Wait a moment.

等一下。

track 239

★ I'm sick of it.

這件事真是煩透了！

深入分析

當你「對某事感到厭煩」時，就非常適合用"be sick of..."的句型，例如你可以說："I'm sick of eating hamburgers."，表示「我厭煩了老是吃漢堡」這件事。

此外，"be sick of"後面要加名詞或動名詞，不可加原形動詞。

實用會話

A Are you OK?

你還好吧？

B I'm sick of it.

真件事真是讓我煩透了！

實用會話

A I'm sick of always waiting for you!

你老讓我等你，真是煩透了。

B I'm so sorry about this.

我對此非常抱歉(遺憾)。

徹底學會英文

I can't take it anymore.

我真的受不了啦！

程度比厭煩(be sick of...)更令人感到生氣或憤怒等，就可以說："I can't take it anymore."

A：It doesn't work.

沒有發揮作用。

B：Oh, my God. I can't take it anymore.

喔，天啊！我真的受不了啦！

track 240

★I can't afford a new car.

我買不起一部新車。

深入分析

若是經濟狀況無法負擔某一項支出或花費，而你又不願意承認"I'm poor."（我很窮），你就可以暗示地說："I can't afford it."，表示「我負擔不起！」

實用會話

Ⓐ Why don't you buy a new car?
你怎麼不買一部新車？

Ⓑ I wish I could, but I can't afford a new car.
我希望我可以，但是我買不起一部新車。

實用會話

Ⓐ They moved to a new apartment last month.
他們上個月搬到新的公寓了！

Ⓑ No kidding. I don't know how he can afford an apartment.
不是開玩笑的吧！我不知道他怎麼負擔得起住公寓的開銷。

track 241

★I really worry about you.

我真的很擔心你！

深入分析

當你擔心朋友的狀況時，就非常適合用"worry"這個字，表示感到憂慮、不安的意思。

實用會話

Ⓐ I really worry about you.

我真的很擔心你！

Ⓑ Come on, everything will be all right.

不用擔心！一切都會很順利的。

實用會話

Ⓐ Will you be all right walking home?

你走路回家沒問題吧？

Ⓑ Don't worry. I'll be fine.

不用擔心！我可以的！

實用會話

Ⓐ We were very worried when he did not answer his phone.

他沒有接電話讓我們很擔心。

Ⓑ I'm sure he'll come back by midnight.

我相信他會在午夜前回來的！

track 242

★I hope I didn't do it.

真希望我沒做那件事。

深入分析

當你後悔自己的行為時，除了說"I'm sorry."之外，你還可以好好反省自己不適當的行為，例如你可以說："I hope I didn't do it."(真希望我沒做那件事)，後面的子句是過去式時態，表示你是針對過去的行為感到懺悔！

實用會話

Ⓐ I hope I didn't do it.

真希望我沒做那件事。

Ⓑ It's not your fault. You have no choice.

不是你的錯！你是毫無選擇啊！

實用會話

Ⓐ I hope she didn't come back.

我真希望她沒回來。

Ⓑ It's all over now.

事情都過去了！

全民學英文
53

How do you do最實用的生活英語

雅致風靡　典藏文化

親愛的顧客您好，感謝您購買這本書。即日起，填寫讀者回函卡寄回至本公司，我們每月將抽出一百名回函讀者，寄出精美禮物並享有生日當月購書優惠！想知道更多更即時的消息，歡迎加入"永續圖書粉絲團"

您也可以選擇傳真、掃描或用本公司準備的免郵回函寄回，謝謝。

傳真電話：（02）8647-3660　　　電子信箱：yungjiuh@ms45.hinet.net

姓名：　　　　　　　　性別：　□男　□女

出生日期：　年　月　日　電話：

學歷：　　　　　　　　職業：

E-mail：

地址：□□□

從何處購買此書：　　　　　　購買金額：　　元

購買本書動機：□封面　□書名　□排版　□內容　□作者　□偶然衝動

你對本書的意見：

內容：□滿意□尚可□待改進　　編輯：□滿意□尚可□待改進

封面：□滿意□尚可□待改進　　定價：□滿意□尚可□待改進

其他建議：

您可以使用以下方式將回函寄回。

您的回覆，是我們進步的最大動力，謝謝。

① 使用本公司準備的免郵回函寄回。

② 傳真電話：（02）8647-3660

③ 掃描圖檔寄到電子信箱：

yungjiuh@ms45.hinet.net

沿此線對折後寄回，謝謝。

廣告回信
基隆郵局登記證
基隆廣字第056號

221-03

雅典文化事業有限公司　收

新北市汐止區大同路三段194號9樓之1

雅致風靡　典藏文化